CONTENTS

KUMA KUMA KUMA BEAR

NOVEL
6

WRITTEN BY
Kumanano

ILLUSTRATED BY
029

Seven Seas Entertainment

KUMA KUMA KUMA BEAR Vol. 6
© KUMANANO 2017

Illustrated by 029

Originally published in Japan in 2017 by
SHUFU TO SEIKATSU SHA CO., LTD., Tokyo.
English translation rights arranged with
SHUFU TO SEIKATSU SHA CO., LTD., Tokyo,
through TOHAN CORPORATION, Tokyo.

Seven Seas press and purchase enquiries can be sent to
Marketing Manager Lianne Sentar at press@gomanga.com.
Information regarding the distribution and purchase of
digital editions is available from Digital Manager CK Russell
at digital@gomanga.com.

Follow Seven Seas Entertainment online at
sevenseasentertainment.com.

TRANSLATION: Jan Cash & Vincent Castaneda
ADAPTATION: M.B. Hare
COVER DESIGN: Kris Aubin
INTERIOR LAYOUT & DESIGN: Clay Gardner
COPY EDITOR: Kelly Lorraine Andrews
PROOFREADER: Stephanie Cohen, Meg van Huygen
LIGHT NOVEL EDITOR: Nibedita Sen
PREPRESS TECHNICIAN: Rhiannon Rasmussen-Silverstein
PRODUCTION MANAGER: Lissa Pattillo
MANAGING EDITOR: Julie Davis
ASSOCIATE PUBLISHER: Adam Arnold
PUBLISHER: Jason DeAngelis

ISBN: 978-1-64827-939-3
Printed in Canada
First Printing: June 2021
10 9 8 7 6 5 4 3 2 1

Skills

▶ FANTASY WORLD LANGUAGE
The fantasy world's language will sound like
    Japanese.
Spoken words are conveyed to the other party in the
    fantasy world language.

▶ FANTASY WORLD LITERACY
The ability to read the fantasy world writing.
Written words become the fantasy world's words.

▶ BEAR EXTRADIMENSIONAL STORAGE
The white bear's mouth opens into infinite space. It
    can hold (eat) anything.
However, it cannot hold (eat) living things.
Time will stop for objects that are inside of it.
Anything that is put into the extradimensional
    storage can be pulled out at any time.

▶ BEAR IDENTIFICATION
By looking through the bear eyes on the Bear Clothes'
    hood, one can see the effects of a weapon or tool.
Doesn't work without wearing the hood.

▶ BEAR DETECTION
Using the wild abilities of bears, can detect monsters
    or people.

▶ BEAR MAP 2.0
Any area looked at by the bear eyes can be made
    into a map.

▶ BEAR SUMMONING
Bears can be summoned from the bear gloves.
A black bear can be summoned from the black glove.
A white bear can be summoned from the white glove.

▶ BEAR TRANSPORTER GATE
By setting up a gate, can move between gates.
When more than three gates are in place, can travel
    to a location by picturing it.
This gate can only be opened with the bear hand.

▶ BEAR PHONE
Can have long-distance conversations with others.
Phone persists until caster dispels it. Physically
    indestructible.
Can call people a bear phone is given to by picturing
    the person.
Incoming call is announced by the sound of a bear's cry.

Magic

▶ BEAR LIGHT
Mana collected in the bear glove creates a light in
    the shape of a bear.

▶ BEAR PHYSICAL ENHANCEMENT
Routing mana through the bear gear allows for
    physical enhancement.

▶ BEAR FIRE MAGIC
Based on the mana that is gathered in the bear glove,
    gives the ability to use fire elemental magic.
Power is proportional to mana and the mental image.
When imagining a bear, power increases even more.

▶ BEAR WATER MAGIC
Based on the mana that is gathered in the bear glove,
    gives the ability to use water elemental magic.
Power is proportional to mana and the mental image.
When imagining a bear, power increases even more.

▶ BEAR WIND MAGIC
Based on the mana that is gathered in the bear glove,
    gives the ability to use wind elemental magic.
Power is proportional to mana and the mental image.
When imagining a bear, power increases even more.

▶ BEAR EARTH MAGIC
Based on the mana that is gathered in the bear glove,
    gives the ability to use earth elemental magic.
Power is proportional to mana and the mental image.
When imagining a bear, power increases even more.

▶ BEAR HEALING MAGIC
Can give treatment by means of the bear's kind heart.

🐻 Equipment

▶ **BLACK BEAR GLOVE (NONTRANSFERABLE)**
Attack glove, increases power based on the user's level.

▶ **WHITE BEAR GLOVE (NONTRANSFERABLE)**
Defense glove, increases defense based on the user's level.

▶ **BLACK BEAR SHOE (NONTRANSFERABLE)**

▶ **WHITE BEAR SHOE (NONTRANSFERABLE)**
Increases speed based on the user's level.
Prevents fatigue when walking long distances based on the user's level.

▶ **BLACK AND WHITE BEAR CLOTHES (NONTRANSFERABLE)**
Appears to be a onesie. Reversible.
FRONT: BLACK BEAR CLOTHES
Increases physical and magic resistance based on the user's level.
Gives heat and cold resistance.
REVERSE: WHITE BEAR CLOTHES
Automatically restores health and mana while worn.
Amount and speed based on the user's level.
Gives heat and cold resistance.

▶ **BEAR UNDERWEAR (NONTRANSFERABLE)**
Won't get dirty no matter how much they're used.
An excellent item that won't retain sweat or smells.
Will grow with the user.

KUMA
KUMA
KUMA
BEAR

121
The Bear Goes to the Royal Capital

BOTH FINA AND SHURI enjoyed seeing the ocean for the first time. They played on the beach, rode on a ship, dug up some bamboo shoots together, and even got to eat Deigha's seafood cooking. But, at last, it was time for the three of us to go back home to Crimonia.

They thanked me again the moment we got back.

"That was fun. Thank you so much, Yuna!" said Fina.

"Thank you, Yuna," Shuri said.

"No problem. Let's go again sometime, eh?"

"Yeah!"

"Yippee!"

They were ecstatic. Now that I thought about it, next time we could go when it was warm enough to swim. Yeah, I'd want to bring the orphans along, too, for sure.

In the meantime, Fina and Shuri's smiles really made me happy. Taking them along...yeah, I'd made the right choice.

From there, I headed over to Tiermina to return what I'd borrowed. That's the trick to long-term relationships, you know? Gotta return borrowed stuff.

"Here, you can have these two back if you want 'em." I gestured at Fina and Shuri.

"We're back, Mom!" Fina and Shuri hugged Tiermina.

Tiermina stroked their heads. "Did you two have fun?"

"Yeah, tons! The ocean was so big. We even got to ride a boat."

"The ocean was salty."

Tiermina laughed. "Well, it *is* saltwater."

The two of them talked on and on about the trip, and Tiermina happily listened. Great stuff, having a close family. It would've been nice if Gentz could be there too, but he was still at the adventurers' guild like the breadwinner he was, working his butt off for the wife and kids.

"Yuna, thank you so much," said Tiermina. "My daughters are going to treasure this forever, I'm sure."

"Why don't you come along with us next time?"

"You know what? Maybe I will."

Around then, the exhaustion caught up with Fina and Shuri—either due to the trip or because they were finally home. They could barely keep their eyes open.

"Heh, aren't you two sleepy?" I said. "I'll get you up when dinner is ready, so go rest."

"Okay. Thanks, Yuna."

"No problem. Just take it easy."

Fina took Shuri's hand and led her to their room. Once Tiermina and I were alone, I told her about the Anz situation. I let her know we'd have more people working in the new shop, and that those women would be coming over once the tunnel was done.

"You just want me to keep an eye on them when they get here, then?"

There was no telling whether or not I'd be in Crimonia when Anz arrived, so I'd told her to go straight to the orphanage. As long as I let Tiermina know about that ahead of time, things would work out. "If I'm not here, just take her to the shop, ask what she needs for it, and get it all ready for her."

"You won't be here?"

"I'm planning on heading to the capital for a bit, so I might not." It wasn't like I *wanted* to go, but I still had that gig guarding students for Ellelaura. I had no clue when the tunnel would be done, but those events *could* coincide.

"You sure are busy, Yuna. Don't push yourself too hard." Tiermina looked toward the second floor, where her daughters slept peacefully. "Those two would be beside themselves if anything were to happen to you."

"I won't do anything dangerous, so it should be all right."

"Says the girl who thinks killing tigerwolves and black vipers somehow isn't dangerous."

"That only happens every once in a while. And there were kids in trouble..."

Tiermina laughed. "I'm joking, Yuna, just, really, though. Don't do anything dangerous."

"Yes, ma'am," I replied obediently, and we got down to brass tacks about what to do when Anz arrived.

I didn't have much time to relax after getting back from Mileela. Soon the day of Ellelaura's job came and blew away what little chill I'd managed to find. I really wasn't feeling it, but a promise was a promise, so I headed to the capital through my bear transport gate to get on with it.

The quest was to guard students while they were doing some hands-on training. Annoying enough, but I was *also* basically guarding people the same age as me. Not great. Ellelaura and the king said they'd vouch for me, but I doubted the students would be cooperative about accepting a girl in a bear onesie for a guard. Sure, they might *say* they were okay with it, but who knew what would really be going on in their sneaky little minds?

I'd gone with the flow at that time, but I wish I could've Bear Time Traveled or something to stop myself from taking the job. (Come on, onesie, please? No?) Anyway, the only saving grace was that Shia would be there.

I got to the capital and headed to Ellelaura's house, the gaze of passersby weighing on me as they always did in the capital. Of course, I didn't have a totally stare-free life in Crimonia either, but I spent enough time there that it wasn't *this* bad.

"Miss Yuna, it has been too long." The maid, Surilina, greeted me when I arrived at the estate. She led me to a room where I met Ellelaura.

"Yuna, you came!"

"As promised. This whole thing's tomorrow, yeah?"

"Oh, I'm glad you remembered. You hadn't come by in a while, so I worried you might have forgotten." (Ugh, I wish I had. That's why I'd waited until the last minute.) "I'm glad you came. Shia was simply ecstatic that you'd be her guard."

"She was?"

"Oh, yes. Surilina went to go get her just now, so she should be right along."

And just as Ellelaura said this, Shia came into the room with her pigtails swinging back and forth. "Mother, is Yuna really here?" Our eyes met. "Yuna! It's been so long. Still wearing that bear outfit, I see! It's cute."

Being called cute by a girl my age felt weird. What, was she trying to treat me like a kid or something? "Been a while since the birthday celebration, huh?"

"It sure has. Now—if you come to the capital, please do also visit our house. I've heard from mother that you've come to the capital on occasion. Supposedly you bring tasty food with you every time."

"Oh, that's for Princess Flora. Ellelaura just pops up out of nowhere, and we end up eating together."

"Mother has an impressive information network." Impressive sure was one way to put it, but I'd rather just call it mysterious. The seventh wonder of the world: the queen's ability to invade my privacy whenever she wanted. "Oh, and how's Noa?"

"She's good. When she sees an opening, she sneaks out of the house and comes to my shop."

"The shop! Yes, I heard from father the other day that you opened one. He said the food is so delicious that it's been thriving. I envy Noa. I'd just love to go back to Crimonia soon," she said with a wistful sigh.

"Still, I never would have thought that *you* would be in

charge of guarding us for this exam, Yuna." Shia really did look ecstatic. Ellelaura wasn't exaggerating.

"Well, Ellelaura asked me. But hey, have the students really accepted having me for a guard?" Apart from Shia, I had my doubts. Who was going to convince them? The king? The queen? Maybe Princess Flora herself? Come on.

"It'll be fine," said Ellelaura. "We made sure to tell them you're a girl prodigy of an adventurer."

"And did you tell them I'm dressed up as a bear?" That had to be the sticking point, right? Any normal person would flip out at that detail.

"Why, ah...well, I haven't told them *that*." Ugh. "Now, I didn't *lie* to them. I made sure to tell the teacher, and the students can take it as they will. But they'll have points deducted from their final score if they insult you, so make sure to report any incidents to us."

Cool. We were looking at a 99.9 to 110 percent chance of vicious teenage mockery. *Love it. Gonna be great for my mental health.* "That's a bit out of line from what you promised."

"I'm sorry. It's just that I—*ahem*—I would like to see the student's reactions when they meet you. Of course, I'll be there the whole time for the introductions, so no need to fret!"

Oh yeah? No need to fret? I was brimming with frets. I was a bear-shaped clearance sale of frets.

Shia blinked. "Umm, so you're going to guard us...in those clothes?"

I mean, I needed the outfit, so... All I could do was nod.

"Everyone was thrilled about having a high-ranking adventurer as our guard. I wasn't surprised, having already heard about you from mother, but everyone else has definitely been given the wrong impression based on what they were told."

What they'd...been told? "Uh. What *did* you tell them, Ellelaura?"

"I told them you became an adventurer at a young age." (Pretty vague, that! They probably weren't thinking I was fifteen, were they?) "I told them that, even though you're a woman, you've slain monsters. Tigerwolves and orcs and worse." Ehh, she wasn't *wrong*. "Everyone's imagined that you're a cool lady."

Okay, what? Cool lady? Me? You know what they say about assumptions. Come on, I'm not a cool lady. I'm a bear!

"Shia is going to follow your lead. After all, she's being graded on mediating interpersonal relationships along with everything else."

Shia groaned. "This is going to be *such* a *nightmare*."

"That's why we call it an exam, dear. Besides, you have an advantage: You know about the contents of the exam in advance."

An advantage? Well...maybe. But even if you could cook up the right answer to a problem, you still had to remember the right formula to get there. What I would *really* need Shia for would be to keep me from exploding and tossing the twerps into a goblin's nest.

"I'm not allowed to talk about how I know Yuna either, am I?" Shia mused. "You're shorter than me and dressed as a cute bear. How am I supposed to back you up?"

How was I supposed to know? If she had a complaint, she could direct it to her mother.

"Those who lead," said Ellelaura, "sometimes find themselves protecting forbidden subjects of conversation. Take that to heart. Find a way to maintain your relations without making anyone upset or uncomfortable. As a daughter of the aristocracy, you must endeavor to honor this truth."

It definitely would be hard for Shia to cope with the students who didn't know about me. I mean, when I first met Shia, she'd thought I was so unbelievable that she challenged me to a duel without warning. Which I brought up right then, by the way.

"What else was I supposed to think? Some adorable-looking bear girl coming out of nowhere, claiming to be protecting Noa? Anyway, it was mother who pushed us to have a match."

Ellelaura tilted her head. "If I hadn't, you wouldn't have believed me. Don't you think?"

"I suppose so..." Shia pouted slightly.

I cleared my throat, gave it plenty of phlegm for emphasis. "Whelp! Looks like this is going to really mean trouble for Shia, so can I just, uh. Not?"

Ellelaura smiled. "No."

Shia and I sighed simultaneously. I half-wanted to say sorry for all the trouble, but it wasn't my fault. Blame the smirking spymaster mom, thank you very much.

"So, where are the lot of us going?" I asked, having accepted my dark fate. I knew I'd be guarding them for multiple days, but not much more than that.

"It's a village some ways out, no more than a two-day ride by carriage. You'll be transporting luggage and flour. Back and forth, I suppose you'll be looking at four, perhaps five days."

Hmm. But if we used Kumayuru and Kumakyu, we could do a round trip in a single day, right? Or would I be allowed to use Kumayuru and Kumakyu? I would much rather ride my bears for any kind of travel…

"We'd travel by carriage then?" I looked as uninterested as possible, and… "Very good, I love it. But, you know, say that I might maybe use Kumayuru and Kumakyu? Or something?"

"Hmm, I really can't condone that. It would be an issue if the students assumed the bears would protect them. On a related note, please hide how strong you really are in front of them."

No bears, then. "What if they're cubs?"

"Cubs?"

Even if I couldn't use my bears for transportation, they could still sense danger. I'd rather have 'em out there at night just in case. I summoned my bears in their cub forms right in front of the two to demonstrate.

"Wh-what?!" Ellelaura almost stumbled back.

"They're so cuuuuUUUUUTE," said Shia, transforming into a siren before my eyes.

Ellelaura and Shia immediately got in on that good, good bear hugging from Kumayuru and Kumakyu, respectively.

"Wait," said Ellelaura, looking up from the cuddly fur for a moment, "are these Kumayuru and Kumakyu's cubs?"

Well, I saw how they would think that. "No, they're original recipe. Kumayuru and Kumakyu, but tiny. My summons are special, so I can miniaturize them." Not that I always could, but they didn't need to know that.

"Well, if they're just itty bitty guys..." (Ellelaura struggled to maintain her composure) "...in the sense that they won't impact the scenario, given their small and cuddly presence, then I see no reason *not* to... Oh, come here, you little sweetie!"

So, I couldn't bring the full-sized versions of my buddies, but I did get permission to use them at cub size. Cool—I'd secured a place for my fluffballs!

After that, the two of them wouldn't let go of the cubbified Kumayuru and Kumakyu until I headed home.

122
The Bear Goes to the Academy

THE NEXT DAY, I dragged my heavy feet to Ellelaura's home.

"Good morning, Yuna," she said sweetly. "Oh goodness, you don't look well."

Oh? Did I not? And whose fault was that? The dark road ahead weighed upon my bearish soul. My carefree trip to the beach with Fina and Shuri was but a distant memory.

"Lovely. I'll take you to the academy."

"Is Shia not around?" I didn't see her.

"Shia went ahead. You'll see her with the other students when you're introduced as their guard." Fine. I supposed that might as well happen. The two of us headed out.

Must've been pretty close, since we saw students wearing uniforms walking around here and there—the same one Shia was wearing when I met her. I'd seen them occasionally while walking around the capital. Cute-looking blazer outfit. We joined a crowd of students and walked to the academy with them.

The students shot glances at me. At this point it was too late, but man...would've been nice to have a carriage. We stood out like red paint on a white cat. Ellelaura didn't seem to mind as she walked beside me, but how could she? I walked a lonely road. The only road that I had ever known...

I pulled my bear hood low over my head and hid my face.

I could hear the students all around me, yammering on and on...

"A bear?"

"Why is a bear going to the school?"

"What's with that weird getup?"

"Is that Lady Ellelaura next to it?"

"What's the bear got to do with Lady Ellelaura?"

"Maybe she's a friend of Lady Shia's?"

"It's cute, but that look is embarrassing."

"Whoa, first time I've seen anything as funny as that."

"Maybe it's for a play?"

"Isn't she embarrassed?"

"I think it's cute."

"Look at the hands. They're bears."

"If we're talking about that, look at the feet."

"Where could anyone even buy that?"

"Well, it might be kind of cute."

"Think she'll eat us if we get too close?"

"I want to give her a hug."

"Yup, that's cute."

"Who would even walk around in that outfit?"

"Oh, I've seen her walking around in it before."

"I heard about her from someone else."

"Can I go home?" I offered.

Ellelaura grabbed me around my arm like she was trying to keep me from making a break for it. "Of course not."

I could've broken free if I really tried, but I couldn't just do something like that to a normal person like Ellelaura and not end up in some kinda court of law for the crime of hand explosion or whatever, so I had to grin and bear it. "I won't run, so if you could let go of me?"

Ellelaura smiled. "No." She dragged me along and, all the while, murmurs of the word "bear" followed us.

I wanted to go home already.

Just when I was about to run out of HP, we got to the academy. The place was gigantic, like a bunch of school buildings mashed up into a small castle.

"This is the academy, huh? It's huge..." I looked up at it.

"It has to be. Expensive as it is, kids in the capital from all walks of life—commoner or aristocrat and everything in-between—all attend."

"Normal people and nobles attend the same academy?"

"Yes. Different curriculums, naturally." I guess they had to have different curricula, with such different futures ahead of them. We had vocational schools even in my original world. We came into a school building, and Ellelaura seemed to suddenly remember something. "Oh, right. Now, Yuna...if you're going to summon Kumayuru and Kumakyu, could you do it here? Having bears appear out of nowhere could give the students a shock."

Fair enough. It would've been a pain to explain my summons, so I called Kumayuru and Kumakyu in their cub forms. ("*Cwoom?*")

With my bears all summoned up, Ellelaura and I headed to a place like a staff room. We were meeting with the homeroom teacher first, I guess.

Just imagining the staff room got me down for some reason. I don't know. I guess I hadn't been attending school before I got here. Maybe that was it? Anyway, I was led over to a man in the staff room, some guy who must've been in his thirties.

Ellelaura nodded. "Mr. Shoog."

"Why, if it isn't Lady Ellelaura, and...uh...*bear*?"

Clearly he meant *bears,* because there were two of 'em: Kumayuru and Kumakyu. Just a little grammatical slip-up. Obviously.

"This girl is Yuna. She's the adventurer I asked to serve as the guard."

The teacher looked between Ellelaura and me. He didn't need to look at me like that for me to know what he wanted to say. "Lady Ellelaura...surely you jest. To my eyes, she appears to be younger than the students she would be guarding..."

I couldn't get too mad at that, but...I was the same age as the students I was gonna guard, even if I was short for my age.

"She is a full-fledged adventurer, and an astounding one on top of that."

The teacher looked at me—small girl in a bear outfit—dubiously. I reluctantly showed him my guild card when Ellelaura told me to.

"Class: Bear?" Hold up, no—it wasn't the class bit that mattered. Come on...

"Please look at the rank," she said.

"Oh, my apologies. C-Rank adventurer. Are you sure? This isn't a counterfeit, is it?"

"It's real. I swear on the name of Ellelaura." A noble swearing on her own name, huh? Did this really call for that?

"If it wasn't you, Lady Ellelaura, I don't know if I'd believe it. And I know, too, that you wouldn't put your own daughter in danger if you didn't trust a young woman like this to guard her."

Nope, this was all wrong. Wasn't he supposed to say, "I find this preposterous, so I can't entrust our important students to her?" Give me an excuse to go home? Any moment now...right? But nope, he trusted Ellelaura all the way with this girl in a bear outfit for...some reason.

He gave back my guild card, which I put into my bear storage.

"Well then...Ms. Yuna, was it? Do you require an explanation of our practical training?"

"All I've heard is that I should only protect them when they're in danger and that I should report on their behavior."

"That's right. But please take their autonomy seriously, understand? Don't intervene even if they head in the wrong direction or take the wrong action. But please do put a stop to anything that could involve any true danger."

Ugggghhhghhhghghgh this was getting to be more and more of a pain. But then, what else could I expect from guarding a bunch of dorks my own age?

He explained the students' assignment just like Ellelaura had the day before.

"So while they're transporting the wheat, I can sleep in the carriage as long as they're not in danger?"

"I suppose so," she mused.

"Lady Ellelaura?" the teacher said.

"That was a joke. Though I do suppose you *will* have time on your hands, as a rule. You can protect them any way you like, Yuna. Do as you please."

The teacher sighed, and at once I sympathized with the guy. Yep. It was just like that with her.

After getting the rundown, Ellelaura and I headed to a classroom where these students I'd be guarding were waiting. We found four of them in their uniforms—two boys and two girls. Shia was one. Looked like these were the students in question.

To summarize, one was a smart-looking boy with long hair, one was a shorthaired boy who looked cocky, one was a pampered-looking princess-type, and the last was Shia.

"A bear?"

"There's a bear here?"

"That *is* a bear, right?"

No, there were *two* bears. Kumayuru and Kumakyu, thank you very much, so...they needed to look at 'em, if they were going to talk about 'em.

"All right," said the homeroom teacher, "quiet down."

"Sir, what is that bear* doing here?"

(*Bears, they definitely meant. Probably Kumayuru and Kumakyu.)

"You're not telling us that she's a member of our party?"

"She's so tiny. Simply unacceptable."

While the students were off talking on their own, Shia, the only person who knew what was up, gave me a small wave so the people around her wouldn't notice.

"No, this bear is—pardon—Yuna, here is—"

Wowwww. He said bear just now, huh? *Just* said it.

The teacher corrected himself and continued, "She is an adventurer who will be guarding all of you."

"Huh? What are you talking about, sir?" said the shorthaired boy. "She's got to be younger than us, just look at her."

(We're talking just a few inches shorter, by the way. I don't know what they were talking about.)

"Yes," added the princess, "I entirely agree. Sir, please do put a stop to these antics."

Oooh, shorthaired boy and the princess were maaad.

"This is no joke," said Ellelaura. "She's a proper adventurer. I went out of my way to ask her to be your guard. You wouldn't do anything to embarrass me, now would you?"

She narrowed her eyes and glared at the students. I still had no idea what kind of position Ellelaura had, but the students shut right up. So she *was* important? Was she? And so she wasn't a spymaster, because...or...? Huh.

"But..."

"Don't worry. I personally guarantee her ability."

Pssh. I wouldn't buy that if I were them, no way. I was a girl who looked younger than anyone in this room, and I was dressed in a bear outfit to boot. Looks do matter, like it or not, and there wasn't a single part of my whole situation that'd seem reassuring.

Which meant I could go home. Maybe. Possibly. Hopefully?

"Lady Ellelaura, is that girl dressed as a bear really an adventurer? Would you let us check her guild card?"

"Hm. My word isn't enough?"

Things were derailing. Was this the point where I'd show them my card so they'd accept me? I dunno. Would that be enough for these guys?

"No," said the student, "I don't mean it in that way, but I want to know for sure."

"Fair enough, I suppose. Yuna, would you mind?"

I took my guild card in my bear puppet's mouth and showed it to everyone.

"Class: Bear."

"That indeed says bear."

"That's a bear."

Nope! Wrong spot. Again!

"Adventurer Rank: C?"

"Rank C?"

"C?"

This time they were looking at the right spot, but they were huddling together.

"Think she's one of *those*?"

"It does look like it."

"She certainly must be."

One of those *what*?

"Lady Ellelaura, if anything happens, we won't need to help her, right? Since she is in Rank C, after all."

"That sounds acceptable."

C'mon, really? No help for a cute little bear?

"As long as we won't be to blame," said one of the boys, "I haven't got any complaints."

"Yeah, man, I'm all right with this too. Besides, I think we could handle an easy practical training exercise like this even without an adventurer guarding us," the other boy said.

No guard? Excuse me, they'd seen my guild card, right? C-Rank adventurer? Cool and capable bear? I looked over at Shia for support and saw her talking with the princess.

"So, Shia, do you think the academy is mocking us? Assigning us a little kid to be our guard and all, I just… well, I suppose it feels like they're making *us* guard *her*."

"She's cute, so why not? Besides, this is such a short distance, so we barely need a guard. I don't think it's anything to worry about."

No, I could use some fellow worriers. I was doing enough worrying on my own, thanks a ton.

"I suppose so. We likely won't be attacked by monsters. I *suppose* I'll accept *this* as *part* of the *practical* training."

Err, she could…keep on not accepting it, actually. Loudly, maybe. To authority figures. So I could go home.

"So, Cattleya, Shia, are you good with this too?"

"I am fine with it."

"Of course, I'm fine with it too."

The princess-y Cattleya and Shia agreed.

Ugh. When was lunch break already?

KUMA
KUMA
KUMA
BEAR

123
The Bear Heads Out for Practical Training

EACH OF THE students introduced themselves to me.
First, we had a shorthaired boy with a good spirit and a bad attitude: Maricks.

Next up, a slightly longhaired, intelligent-looking boy: Timol.

Then we had that princess-y girl, who wore a hairband over her long, silver hair: Cattleya.

Then, finally, there was Ellelaura's daughter Shia.

After some pretty straightforward introductions, Cattleya spoke up. "I've been wondering...what is with those bears?" She looked at Kumayuru and Kumakyu, who were resting by my feet.

"They're mine."

Maricks laughed. "You're bringing your pets? What are you, some kinda princess?"

A princess? *Me*? Besides, Kumayuru and Kumakyu weren't pets. They were family!

They uniformly disregarded my internal torment and left me to trail behind as we departed the academy to board the carriage. This was where the teacher and Ellelaura would be leaving us; the practical training started the moment we exited the classroom.

Along the way, Shia slowed down to my pace and spoke in a low voice. "Yuna, I'm looking forward to working with you. Kumayuru and Kumakyu, too," she said, nodding at the bears trotting along beside us.

"Okay, but, Shia? You gotta help me out there. You're the only one I can rely on."

"Of course."

All I could do now was trust her word. "And hey, what was all that earlier about one of *those*?"

"One of *those*?"

"Yeah, one of *those*." When the three other students saw my guild card, they'd said something like that. I had no clue what they'd meant.

"They probably assumed you're a spoiled girl from somewhere who bought your rank."

Oh, right—someone could just go on quests with high-ranking adventurers to coast by and increase their own rank. In other words, they thought I was some hobby-adventurer pampered princess who'd bought her rank along with a couple of bear pets.

"But if someone tried that, wouldn't the truth spread around to the other adventurers?" I asked. "What would be the point?"

"Well, that's why they've accepted your whole…situation," she said, gesturing vaguely at me. "Because they think you're eccentric and coddled."

Blurgh. Annoying. But then, here I was, a young-looking girl in a bear onesie, supposedly a C-Rank adventurer. That was pretty hard to swallow compared to me just being some bored, LARPing rich girl.

We headed out of the academy and to the back of the school building where we found a small shed. Inside of that shed was a single carriage and a stable.

Maricks scanned the stable with a restless look in his eyes. "I knew it. We're the last ones."

"Last ones?" I asked.

Shia nodded. "There are other parties with their own assignments. Maricks has a contest with the other boys about who comes back the fastest."

Cattleya snorted. "How absurd."

I mean, she wasn't wrong.

"What are you doing?" Maricks snapped. "Hurry up and get ready! Let's roll!" He was practically already climbing inside the carriage when he turned and shouted at us.

The carriage's luggage rack had a roof, hopefully to keep the water away if it rained. There were two horses connected to the carriage—enough to pull it, apparently.

When I headed around to the back and passed by the driver's seat, Maricks called out to me, "I have no idea why you're coming with us, but you know what? Whatever. Just don't get in our way."

"That's right," Timol sneered. "Stay out of our way, and don't even *think* about lowering our assessment result."

Love to deal with crappy, yammering boys. Love it. Ugh...if Shia weren't there, I would've peaced out then and there.

"You're both being rude to Yuna," said Shia. "She's going out of her way to guard us, so make sure to treat her with proper courtesy."

Maricks rolled his eyes. "You want me to play nice with some bear? Just look at her: She's all full of herself because of that phony rank, the little weirdo."

Full of myself?! They were about to shatter my glass heart...

"Maybe protecting her is part of the test?" Timol interjected.

"You think so?" Maricks mused. "You reckon we have to keep her safe?"

"That's one possibility. If protecting her *is* a part of the test, that'd line up with a lot of stuff. They might even have given us false information, so she can report on our actions to the teachers."

"Hey, is that true?" Maricks asked me.

"They just told me I'd be guarding everyone," I said.

"It's possible they didn't tell her either." Timol was developing his own pet theory.

"What a pain. Shia, Cattleya, you take care of the weird girl and the bears. Have some girl time. Talk about clothes and junk."

Cattleya glared. "Who said you could make all the decisions? Why, I—"

"No problem," said Shia quickly. "I'll take care of Yuna and the bears."

Cattleya tilted her head. "Shia?"

"Heh. No take backs, ladies. You *better* actually look after them, since you agreed to it. We're sure not gonna do it."

The two boys smiled like they'd dodged a week full of chores as they headed to the coachbox. Shia had practically the same smile on her own face...for different reasons, I could tell.

"Well then, Yuna, let's board the carriage." Shia pulled me up and we got into the carriage's cargo hold.

There were bags of wheat for the village piled up inside, just like I'd been told about. I looked for an open space to sit down. Kumayuru and Kumakyu came over to my side, then got on my lap.

"I don't mind looking after the bears," said Cattleya uncertainly, "but are you really sure you're all right with this, Shia?"

"Are you, Cattleya? I can look after Yuna by myself, you know."

"Goodness, yes. A fine lady must be able to mind small children, so I don't mind."

But, but looking after *them* was *my* job! We'd reversed roles. All because of that freakin' onesie, I bet...

"Cattleya, thank you."

"Oh, don't worry your sweet little self about it. Now, my tiny bear companion, kindly let us know the moment you require anything, mm?" What confidence she had in me as a guard. Ugh. She'd make this bear so sad she'd bawl her eyes out. "Still, I wonder if they couldn't have let us have a carriage more suitable for refined young women like ourselves," Cattleya murmured, looking around the interior.

"I don't know. I mean, this *is* meant to be a cargo carriage, after all."

"Yes, dear, of *course,* dear, but the thought of spending multiple days in this carriage is most dispiriting to my delicate demeanor."

I was on the same wavelength as Cattleya. No traveling on Kumayuru and Kumakyu and their top-notch, uber-cuddly fur. No using the bear house to sleep for the night. No hot baths or fluffy beds...I was in for a pretty inconvenient trip.

When I looked over at Shia and Cattleya, they were pulling out pillows from their item bags and setting them up to sit on. Aha, cushions *would* soften the jolting. These two were fully prepared.

"Yuna, you can use my cushion, if you'd like." Shia held out the cushion she'd been sitting on. I didn't see any others. Was she trying to lend me her only comfort?

"It's fine. I have one." I pulled out a cushion embroidered with a bear pattern from my bear storage. One of the orphans, Sherry, had given it to me as thanks, and I'd kept it around as a sweet keepsake. I muttered a thanks to Sherry under my breath as I set it up.

"That's a cute cushion." Shia had set up her cushion close to mine.

"Umm, it was Yuna, correct? Not 'bear'?" said Cattleya. "Once again, it is a pleasure to meet you. Let me assure you, dear, that you'll be under sound protection while in our hands. No need to worry, not a whit."

It didn't seem like Cattleya believed the part about me being a C-Rank adventurer, but she was all right. Maybe this trip wouldn't be so bad.

After Shia sat next to me, she started hugging Kumayuru, who was resting in my lap. "It really is just as soft as I expected."

"Um, Yuna? Would you perhaps allow me to touch your bears too?" Cattleya seemed a little embarrassed. When I nodded, she cautiously extended her hand and patted Kumakyu's head. Kumakyu closed its eyes, thoroughly enjoying the pets.

"Gracious, it's so tame."

"Well, as long as you don't hurt them, they won't do anything to you."

"Why, I thought that bears were frightening, but they seem adorable when seen like this."

Cattleya also hugged Kumakyu. Then Shia nabbed Kumayuru from me and Cattleya stole Kumakyu. The bear...was bearless and lonely.

Irrespective of my feelings, Maricks called into the carriage from the coachbox, "All right, we're heading out."

"You may depart anytime," said Cattleya.

"Sounds good," added Shia.

With that, the carriage was off, and before long we were out of the capital.

"All right—we're the ones driving for now, but we'll switch after midday."

Shia hugged Kumayuru, Cattleya hugged Kumakyu, and I was rocked along by the carriage all by myself as we rolled along.

Thanks to my bear outfit, the jolting didn't hurt my bum and the cushion was a snug seat. I really had to thank Sherry for making it. Maybe I'd buy her something in the capital.

The carriage rolled on smoothly, and we took a break for lunch and to rest the horses. Each student pulled out simple meals like bread and stuff from their item bags. Pretty sad-looking, if you asked me. I had tons of hot meals in my bear storage...but it wasn't like I could pull out a steaming hot meal from there in front of 'em, so I went with some sandwiches that Morin had made.

There were tons of different kinds: egg, cheese, veggie, potato salad, and meat. Naturally, every single one of Morin's sandwiches was delicious.

"That looks good, Yuna." Shia peeked at my sandwiches.

"Want some?"

"Are you sure?"

"It's fine. I have a ton. And you over there—Cattleya, right? You want one too?"

"May I really?" She was looking at them covetously. I handed her one. Cattleya thanked me, brought it to her mouth, and... "It's so delicious. Why, this is even better than my family chef's!"

"I bet. This baker's brilliant," I said. It kind of felt like Cattleya was praising me, honestly, which felt fantastic.

As the three of us made short work of the sandwiches, Maricks looked over at us from his spot a little farther away. When I looked at him, though, he turned right around. Weird.

We finished our break, and the girls took over driving. Obviously, I wasn't about to suffer through staying in the cabin with the boys, so I headed toward the coachbox with Shia and Cattleya.

The three of us somehow managed to all fit up there. Shia grabbed the reins and I sat to her right, nabbing a big ol' hug from Kumayuru—I'd finally managed to get my bear back.

As for Kumakyu, it rested in Cattleya's lap. *Looks like she made a new friend.*

KUMA
KUMA
KUMA
BEAR

124
The Bear Worries About How Much She Can Say

THE SUN BEGAN TO SET, so Shia and the others started prepping to camp. Wasn't much work to do, though—they just took care of the horses and set up a fire. Each of us had already eaten separately, so all we had to do was get to bed.

"All right," said Maricks, "the night watch is going to be in this order: I'll be up first, then Timol, Cattleya, and Shia. We all good?"

Nods all around. Since he didn't say my name, I guess that meant I could sleep.

Maricks sat in front of the fire to start his night watch. Shia and Cattleya went inside the carriage.

"Timol, are you quite sure about this?" Cattleya asked— but Timol was already prepping to sleep outside.

"No way am I going to sleep near some girls. I'll sleep out here with Maricks."

"I'm quite grateful for that," said Cattleya with a polite nod. "I would have just as much trouble sleeping with boys around."

The three of us staked out our sleeping spots in the cramped carriage. When we were all lying down, we barely fit...and I bet Timol had figured as much. Clever guy.

Shia and Cattleya used the narrow space they had to wrap themselves in blankets and lie down. Me, I spread out my blanket and called Kumayuru and Kumakyu. They waddled happily over to me. Sure, they weighed down on my stomach, but my bear outfit made sure it didn't feel heavy. They were just fluffy.

"I'm so jealous, Yuna"

"Gracious me, I am too. Who wouldn't want such cute bears?"

"I know I would."

Kumayuru and Kumakyu poked their heads out of my blanket, and the girls gazed at them jealously. I hugged Kumayuru and Kumakyu close.

"Hey, girls, hurry up and get some sleep," said Maricks from outside. "We're not gonna wait for you to rest up before it's your shift, got me?" Cattleya and Shia quickly pulled up their blankets.

"Well, everyone," said Cattleya, "please sleep well."

Shia smiled. "Good night, Cattleya, Yuna."

"Yup, night."

I thought we'd get in a little girl talk, but it seemed they were tired from traveling—they were snoring right away. *I guess we can't all be bearish globetrotters, huh?*

I didn't change into my white bear clothes—what if they laughed at me, you know? And anyway, I hadn't used any mana or done anything that would have worn me out. If I *was* tired, it was all mental. Turned out that boys my age were a bunch of exhausting babies. That's the thing about being a shut-in all your life who suddenly has to be around people: You get to catch up on a lot of *fun* everyday experiences.

I gave Kumayuru and Kumakyu a serious look while I hugged 'em. "Let me know if monsters or bandits show up... And I don't think it'll happen, but if those boys try any funny business? Lemme know so I can explode them."

Kumayuru and Kumakyu let out their tiniest "cwooms." (Didn't want to wake the other two, after all.) I used them in place of a body pillow. Perfectly warm, perfectly fuzzy, perfectly comforting... And in a snap, I was out.

Didn't take long before I felt someone moving. I opened my eyes slightly to find Cattleya standing up for her guard duty shift.

"I will head over this moment," she said softly to someone else—probably Timol. Cattleya got off the carriage, I hugged Kumayuru, and I was out like a light again. Before long, Cattleya came back and woke up Shia. Since Shia was last, that meant it would be morning soon. Shia got out of the carriage, Cattleya wrapped herself in a blanket, and she was out again.

Carefully, quietly, I got up and managed not to wake Cattleya. Kumayuru and Kumakyu poked their heads out from the blanket as if to ask what I was up to. I picked 'em up, blankets and all, and got out of the carriage.

"Yuna, what's the matter?" Shia asked me softly.

"I'm the only one who didn't get a shift. Felt weird, so I figured I'd keep you company." I sat down beside her.

"Thank you," she said. She shivered a little and held her hands out to the fire.

"Cold?"

"A little." The sun hadn't come up yet, so I supposed

it would be cold. Bear gear and all made that hard to tell—not to mention the heaters in my blanket.

I pulled Kumayuru out of the blanket and handed the bear over to Shia. Kumayuru cocked its head to the side and looked at me.

"Hey, little guy, can you warm Shia up a little?"

"Are you sure?" Shia said, but she still reached out toward me. Kumayuru let out a small "cwoom" as Shia gave it a hug and pulled it into her blanket. "It's warm. Thank you, Yuna. Thank you too, Kumayuru."

She gave Kumayuru a joyful little hug, and I gave Kumakyu one too.

"Your big bears are adorable, but the small ones are too."

No surprise there: They were baby animals, after all, and all of those guys are tiny and adorable. No exceptions to the rule! Baby lions, and tigers, and bears...

"Oh my, this is almost too comfy. I'm getting sleepy." Shia closed her eyes, looking like she was on cloud nine.

"Don't fall asleep."

"I know, but now I can brag to Noa."

"Brag about what?"

"Noa was bragging about how she cuddled your bears till she fell asleep. She was so smug about, too. Who wouldn't be annoyed?"

Was this a normal sibling rivalry thing? Weird.

Shia buried her face into Kumayuru. "Ohhh, this is so nice! Heh."

"I mean it, don't you dare fall asleep."

Shia yawned a lot while hugging Kumayuru, but she managed to stand guard against the things in the night *and* her own drowsiness. Before long, her time was up and so was the sun.

Shia stood. "I'm going to wake everyone up soon." Needless to say, she was still carrying Kumayuru.

After everyone got up, we had a simple breakfast before heading off toward our destination: the village. The mission was a go...

And the mission was super boring. I usually didn't get bored while I was traveling on my bears, but *this* was dull. I could take a nap while riding my bears, but it wasn't like I could sleep in the carriage when I was supposed to be on guard duty, especially if I wanted the students to stop thinking I was useless.

While I was thinking that over, Kumayuru and Kumakyu "cwoom"ed—they were being carried in Shia and Cattleya's arms.

"What's wrong?" asked Shia.

Shia and Cattleya patted Kumayuru and Kumakyu's heads, but they didn't stop crooning.

Cattleya frowned. "Yuna, Kumayuru and Kumakyu started whining all of a sudden."

I took my bears. They looked at me, then in the direction the carriage was headed.

There weren't monsters around, were there?!

I used my detection skill and checked the surroundings. Yeah—there were goblin signals in the direction the carriage was headed. Five in all, and no way to dodge 'em.

What was I supposed to do in a situation like this? I could tell them, keep my mouth shut, or even take care of the baddies for the students. But Shia and company could fight off five measly goblins, right? And I *had* been told not to intervene—but also to guard them?

Ugh, what was I supposed to do?

"Yuna, what is Kumayuru saying?" asked Shia, snapping me out of my thoughts. Could I even tell her?

Well, Shia was supposed to be supporting me, so maybe it'd be fine if it was just her. I leaned toward Shia's ear and whispered to her so that no one else would hear: "It looks like Kumayuru and Kumakyu spotted some nearby monsters."

"Monsters... They can tell?" Shia looked at Kumayuru and Kumakyu in surprise.

To be more accurate, I'd been the one to pinpoint the monster's location with my detection, but Kumayuru and

Kumakyu *had* spotted the monsters first. So... "Pretty much. They're special."

Shia accepted that. They *were* summons and they *could* change sizes, so that fit with everything else.

"This is supposed to be training and all, so I wasn't sure who to tell," I told her. It wasn't like I was a teacher or anything, so I didn't know what to do when weaker monsters appeared. If these were orcs, on the other hand, I'd have a better answer.

"And you're certain?"

I nodded. My detection skill informed my own eyes and indicated goblins, but Shia couldn't see what I could.

Shia nodded. "All right. I think you're not supposed to tell us, but you want the others to trust you. I think it'd be good to say something this time."

"You sure?"

"Yeah. I think it's better for everyone to know if Kuma-yuru and Kumakyu can spot monsters. What if we get into a real emergency later and the others don't believe you?"

How many emergencies actually cropped up on a round trip from the capital to a nearby village? As a rule, the monster encounter rate between towns was low, what with all the wandering adventurers who killed 'em, which made situations like this pretty unusual.

Shia stood and called out to Maricks and the others up front. "It looks like there are monsters nearby. Maricks, stop the carriage!"

Maricks brought the carriage to a halt, startled. "What! Monsters?! Where?!" Maricks swung his head left and right, checking the surroundings.

"There aren't any around yet. Apparently they're up ahead."

"Up ahead?! I don't see any." Maricks squinted forward, but he wouldn't be able to see them—they were too far, and a little off to the right.

"Yuna's bears said there were monsters," Shia said sensibly.

"Uh-huh. To be clear, you're talking about the bears that *that* bear is holding?" Maricks gave me a dubious look. "Really?"

"Yep. Up ahead on the right."

Maricks gave Kumayuru a skeptical look.

"Maricks," said Timol, "animals have a good sense of smell. Maybe that's how they know." There we go, Timol—coming in with the save.

"Hm. Okay. Let's keep an eye on our surroundings while we advance, yeah?"

Everyone nodded in agreement. He gripped the reins and drove the carriage forward.

"Yuna," asked Marick from up front, "your bears are able to do that?"

"Basically. These cubs can warn me about danger, so they can be guards."

"Pretty amazing pets for such a mediocre person," said Maricks. Because I'd said that Kumayuru was the one to detect the monsters, huh? Ugh, so much for trying to show how useful I was.

"Maricks, don't say it like that," Timol mumbled.

"What, am I wrong?"

Come one, come all, and see the incompetent bear and her hyper-competent pets! Ah well... Even if they just trusted Kumayuru and Kumakyu, they'd still listen next time we ran into any danger. That was enough for now.

"So just to confirm," I said to Shia and Cattleya, "you can handle goblins and wolves, right?"

"Yes, if there aren't too many," said Shia. "We should be fine handling monsters like those."

"Yes, I could certainly defeat a goblin."

Well, that was reassuring. "Gotcha. I'll only step in if it gets dangerous, all right?"

"Quit trying to pull our legs!" Maricks whined from up front. "We don't need help from a bear like you. We can handle a few monsters on our own. Your little bears can keep watch, if you wanna feel useful."

At least he didn't say he could solo it. *Good job, Maricks: You mentioned literally anyone else in your calculations. You even knew the most obvious fact about combat: That it's easier to fight together instead of recklessly plowing forward.*

Well, fine. There were only five goblins this time, so I could just spectate. This was practical training, so I wasn't supposed to intervene much.

Time to see just how practical Maricks was.

The carriage continued along. We were close.

"Maricks, look," said Timol. We could see five figures ahead and to the right—the goblins.

Maricks stopped the carriage and stared at the goblins like he couldn't believe it. "Just like the bear said..."

"What should we do, Maricks?" Shia said, bringing Maricks back down to earth.

"We'll, uh, split into two groups. Timol and I will attack from the right, Shia and Cattleya from the left."

Everyone nodded.

"Well, Yuna, I'm heading over," Shia said.

Maricks got down from the carriage and the others

climbed out after him. Wait, was everyone leaving? What about the carriage? I couldn't drive a carriage. What if the horses started moving on their own?

I'd been left behind. They'd handed the reins off to me and there I sat, holding them limply, watching the four of them wander off toward the goblins. Just me, a carriage, some horses, and my anxiety.

Ugh, what if the goblins got too close and spooked the horses? It'd be chaos...

"Kumayuru, Kumakyu, can you drive the carriage?" I asked, just in case.

"Cwoom..."

"I figured. You don't have to rub it in, though."

It was almost funny: I was way more terrified of being in the driver's seat of a carriage than in the middle of a gang of goblins.

Good horseys. Peaceful horseys...nice, calm, extremely immobile horseys...

125
The Bear Watches the Students

MARICKS'S GROUP didn't exactly go in stealthily; the goblins noticed, and the students readied their weapons.

From what I'd heard, Maricks couldn't use magic much, so he mained with a sword. Timol, on the other hand, preferred magic. Shia and Cattleya were pretty good at both. Plan was for Maricks, Shia, and Cattleya to take the lead, with Timol in the rear guard.

The goblins held thick tree branches—nothing too bad, if you could avoid getting hit. They broke into a snarling sorta laugh at the sight of the students, this awful "Ghee ghee ghee ghee."

Praying that the horses wouldn't get spooked, I watched the students engage.

Maricks, Shia, and Cattleya ran forward. Mid-dash, Shia and Cattleya fired off wind magic, throwing a cloud of dust at the goblins. The goblins growled (that nasty "ghee ghee ghee ghee") and closed their eyes, swinging their sticks at random. Maricks closed in on the goblins and—slash—a goblin arm went flying. Shia and Cattleya followed his lead, and Timol kept blasting magic from the back for cover fire.

The fight was going smoothly. Maybe they'd been taught to blind monsters using wind at school? I mean, I'd have just gone full decapitation-a-thon from the start and been done with it, but maybe Shia and Cattleya couldn't do that?

I hadn't seen other people's magic very often, so I didn't know how strong they were on average. Even after coming to this world, I was still a loner. Which was fine, of course. I had bear equipment. I didn't need anything else, or anyone.

The battle went on, and the students were doing great. I'd thought they *might* need my help, but they were really cleaning up. Sure, the goblins had numbers, but Shia's group knew what they were doing. Maricks was getting in the fatal blows, and Timol kept on blasting to keep 'em occupied.

Ellelaura was right: They could handle a couple of goblins.

A goblin swung its dinky wooden stick at Maricks, but (clack!) Maricks caught it with his sword, setting up a perfect (and way brutal) backstab from Cattleya.

"Shia, there's one more."

"On it."

Shia gathered mana in her hand and tossed a fireball at the goblin. The fireball hit the goblin with a vicious sizzle, the thing stopped moving, and Shia brought her sword down on it for good measure without a moment's hesitation.

Whoa. And to think I'd worried.

Maricks smirked. "That was nothing."

Okay, the kids hadn't been in danger, but their magic still seemed weak when they attacked...right? Or was my magic that strong? Then again, normal E-Rank adventurers could slay goblins, so I supposed the students were powerful enough.

The real issue would be orcs. Half-baked abilities wouldn't be enough for one of those pig-heads, so I'd probably have to carry the party in that case. And for all the students' power, there was a lack of experience—not experience *points*, mind you. More like...I saw them hesitate about *how* to attack, like noobs in a game.

In the game world, I'd faced thousands—maybe tens of thousands—of monsters and people. I'd died a lot, lost plenty of times, and built up my experience. Dying and losing were experience, even if you couldn't pin an XP value on 'em. Losing could be knowledge, could tell you what you were lacking and what you needed...but these kids couldn't lose like that. Or, uh, they could lose exactly once before spending their "game over" in a casket. No way to carry that experience forward.

On the other hand, when it came to experience, *I* had no experience handling carriages. I couldn't drive one. Just sitting in the driver's seat made me nervous. Experience was power—physical or mental, experience was growth. If I hadn't stockpiled experience from that game world back then, I think I'd have a hard time even with my bear gear.

Which was the point of the practical training, I supposed. Ellelaura and the king had both said something to that effect, right? Stuff like the hardships that came with travel, horse management, the difficulties of camping, the terror of a monster, the challenge of cooperating with others or establishing trust with a guard. All of that and more. Fighting monsters was just another part of the list.

The kids had to experience it, and I had to make sure they didn't take those experiences to the grave. Yeah, this was gonna be more difficult than I'd thought—I'd have to give Ellelaura a piece of my mind when I got back.

Shia smiled sweetly. "You didn't actually believe there were goblins, right?"

"Yeah," Maricks admitted.

"That proves it then, hmm? Those bears really can detect monsters."

Maricks sighed. "I really can't believe it though."

Everyone looked at Kumayuru and Kumakyu, sitting on either side of me. The bears tilted their heads at the group.

"You sure it wasn't a coincidence?" Maricks continued in a strained voice.

I looked at my bears. I mean, it *was* a pretty wild thing to swallow. The little dudes looked like normal bear cubs. What if some rando back in my old world had told me that his feral squirrels could sense muggers? Would I believe it? Would *you*?

Luckily, I had a spokesperson on my side. "It's not like the bears would lie to us," said Shia.

Multiple spokespersons! (Spokes...people...s?) "Yes, that's right."

Shia and Cattleya scowled at Maricks. He took a step back, then another. Shia and Cattleya took a step forward, then another.

"The bears proved it, didn't they?" said Shia.

"If they really detected the monsters by coincidence, Maricks, then why don't you tell us where all the monsters are, hmm? Use *your* coincidence, why don't you?" Okay, Cattleya was going just a bit overboard.

The two of them took another step toward him.

"Okay, I get it. I believe you. Jeez, fine, I believe everything, just...you don't have to get that mad!"

"Marvelous, Maricks. You finally fit a new idea into that tiny, thick little head of yours," said Cattleya.

Satisfied, the two of them left Maricks alone.

"Still, it's amazing the bears can tell where there are monsters," said Timol, looking over Kumayuru and Kumakyu. (If he had glasses, this would have been the perfect time for him to push them up by the bridge of his nose...but then, wearing glasses into battle would've been a bad idea to begin with.)

"Anyway," Maricks admitted, "that was helpful." From there, he started to give everyone instructions on how to clean up the goblins.

See, goblin corpses can attract monsters. You have to bury or incinerate them, or things'll get hairy. It looked like they'd learned that in school, since they properly disposed of the bodies.

"I must admit," said Cattleya after dealing with them,

"having the bears here during our practical training is such a comfort." She scooped up Kumakyu in her arms and sat down in the driver's seat. I pretended to be reluctant when I handed the reins over to her. I don't think she noticed.

Ugh, finally. Now I could relax even if the horses started losing it. The true battle...was finished.

"I'm not going to tell you about monsters on goblin-level next time, though, you hear me?" I said. "Next time it's all you, and I'm not gonna step in unless you're really in trouble. Consider this a freebie."

"You make an excellent point," said Timol. Maricks and him were climbing up into the carriage. "We must rely on our own strength."

Maricks shrugged. "Bears or no bears, we can take care of some measly goblins. We could take on, like, *twenty* goblins, I bet."

"Is there a hard limit? How many goblins is too many?"

"None! It doesn't matter how many there are!" Maricks responded.

"Really?" Shia broke in. "Because I think we could fight them one-on-one, each of us, and be fine. I think if we were surrounded, we could each handle two or three if we worked really hard, but that would be our limit."

In other words, they could handle double the number of goblins? We were looking at ten-ish then. More than ten, and the bear had to come out of her cave. Fair enough.

Once Maricks and Timol were aboard, we headed out again for the village. We encountered monsters only one more time before we got to our destination. Just four, so I left it to the students. Things went smoother than last time—looked like their experience had already paid off.

The carriage plowed forward until the village came into view up ahead.

With that, we were halfway done.

126
The Bear Tours the Village

THE RESIDENTS WELCOMED us at once. They led our carriage to a place at the center of the village, a sort of public square. Maricks stopped the carriage and got out, followed by Timol, Shia (who was hugging Kumayuru), and Cattleya (who was hugging Kumakyu).

The villagers were amazed by the little bears, but they started outright bustling when I came out.

"A bear?"

"A *bear*?"

"It's a bear."

"Why is she wearing that?"

"Is that the fashion in the capital?"

All kinds of stuff. I pulled my bear hood low to hide... which made the bear ears stand up taller, so I looked even more bear-like. Still, it was better than showing my face.

While that was going on, an elderly man approached us. "Welcome to our fair village, travelers. My name is Kaboss. I am the head of this village."

"I am Maricks from the academy," said Maricks, suddenly our polite representative. "The goods we've brought are in the carriage."

Come to think of it, Maricks *was* the leader of our party. Maricks had been giving directions during the earlier goblin battle, and he'd been the one telling everyone how to keep watch. This stuff happened in the game too; whenever there was a party made up of men and women, some hotshot guy usually ended up becoming party leader.

"Thank you very much," said Kaboss. "We'll take care of your carriage. We have arranged rooms for everyone, so please rest."

The village head pointed, and a man approached the carriage. Timol handed over the reins to him, but the village head looked quizzically at the carriage.

"Is something the matter?" asked Maricks.

"Ah. Well, you see, I thought that there would be an adventurer with you. Did you strapping young folk truly come alone?"

Uh, no? I was right there? Next to him? Did he really mistake me for one of the students? I wasn't even wearing that uniform and navy mantle—I was dressed as a bear. A *bear*! Not exactly standard dress, as far as I knew. Sure, it wasn't exactly adventurer-y, but, c'mon.

"I was told," said old man Kaboss, "that there would be an adventurer serving as your guard."

Shia and the other students looked over in my direction.

"If you're looking for the adventurer, sir..." Maricks cleared his throat and smiled like his lips were being held hostage. "It's her."

"The adventurer is, ah. Her? This adorable bear girl?"

"Yes," said Maricks. "Apparently."

Rude little dork. I'd showed him my guild card! Rank C, and I'd be even higher if I wanted.

The village head looked at me like a side attraction in a traveling freak show. "We had some spirits prepared for the adventurer as part of the reception, but..." The village head looked troubled, which didn't seem fair. I was the one being put on the spot. Was it my fault that I wasn't drinking age?

"Well," said the old man, changing the subject, "what shall we do about your rooms? Would you like to be separate from the students, or would you prefer their company? Naturally, we have separate rooms for the boys and girls, so please don't fret."

The village head gave me an appraising look. I felt like the mystery bag at an auction, but angrier. Sure, a bear onesie had to be unusual, but did he have to look at me like that?

"I don't mind sharing a room with them." If I was with the girls, I could guard Shia and Cattleya. If things somehow broke *real* bad, I'd at least be able to keep them alive.

"Yes, yes. Now: You must be exhausted after traveling from the capital. Please rest, won't you?"

We were led to a house that was larger than the ones around it—the village head's, I supposed. From there, they took us to rooms on the second floor that were split by gender.

"We will call when dinner is ready. Would you kindly rest until then?" With that, the village head ducked out to do old people stuff.

"Gracious, I am exhausted." Cattleya sank down into a chair.

"For sure." Shia also sat down in a chair next to her.

"You, on the other hand, seem positively full of spirit, Yuna!"

"I'm an adventurer." My mouth twitched. "I *am* an adventurer, okay?" I wasn't tired, but that was only because of the bear gear. Without it, I bet I would've been beat from the first day.

"Really, now? You're being honest, Yuna?"

"Yep. I showed you my guild card, didn't I?"

"You did, but... Well, now, don't you and Shia know each other?"

"Err. Don't we what?"

Shia turned away from Cattleya's gaze. I pulled my hood low.

"Lie all you wish, but I'm no fool. Shia, you knew the names of the bears from the start," Cattleya said, holding and patting Kumakyu's head.

"Hh," said Shia.

"Moreover, I can tell by the way you act with Yuna."

"Mm," said Shia.

"You were talking during the night watch, were you not?"

She'd seen right through us. She even knew we'd been keeping watch together.

"Don't say anything to Maricks or Timol," Shia finally said.

"I won't. But tell me this, won't you? Why must I keep this from them?"

"That's...part of the test for the practical training," Shia answered, her voice strained.

"Is it? I hadn't realized. My apologies."

"It's fine. That isn't the only part of the test."

"Right. You must have known about Kumayuru and Kumakyu then, Shia?"

"Uh-huh, I knew about them. And their fuzzy-wuzzy little ears, and their widdle noses..." Shia placed Kumayuru, the bear she was carrying, on the table.

"And their 'widdle' monster detection abilities?"

"No. Yuna didn't say a single world about that." Shia turned her gaze to me—I don't know, I was just sitting on a bed watching it all. Was I supposed to say something, or?

"That's because it was a secret," I said. "Besides, there wasn't a good time to tell you."

"Then, Shia, is Yuna really an adventurer?"

Uh. Yeah? I already said so? Was this about the bear onesie again or was it—

"I leave that for you to decide, Cattleya," said Shia, which was very dramatic and cool and all, and the ambiguity about my abilities was honestly kind of rad, but she could've said that I was an adventurer at least. Right?

Right?

As we rested, the villagers finished prepping and called us down. The table was lined with food prepared by the old man's wife. "We have plenty," she said, "so please eat to your heart's content."

"Thank you very much," said Maricks in his representative voice, and we dug in. Some small talk followed: The village head and his wife simply refused to believe I was an adventurer.

"Well then," he said finally, "would you like a tour around the village tomorrow?"

Apparently, this was part of the assignment after we delivered the payload. Another thing Ellelaura had kept me in the dark about. Students living in the capital never went out to villages, after all, and even daughters of aristocrats like Shia probably didn't go to villages often, so I guess it was educational?

Still, a village tour? I hoped it wouldn't be *too* boring.

We finished our meal and headed back to our rooms to rest, but Kumayuru and Kumakyu weren't with me. Nope—Kumayuru was with Shia, and Cattleya was holding Kumakyu. The both seemed pretty tuckered out. As soon as they got in bed, I could hear them snoring. I couldn't just grab my bears back when they were so comfy, so I ended up sleeping alone.

Ugh. Very alone...

The next day, the village head guided us on a tour through the village.

It wasn't much different from any other village I'd seen. Field. Cattle. Standard vegetables. Bog-standard village, aside from the village kids that were following us.

Apparently they were interested in Kumayuru and Kumakyu, who were still being held by Shia and Cattleya—and by me, too, I guess.

"Pardon them," said old man Kaboss. "It's just that your appearance seems rather unusual. Do people wear clothes like that in the capital?"

"Uh..." Obviously not, right?

"They don't," said Maricks quickly. "There's no one in the capital who dresses like that."

Okay, he didn't have to be so definitive about it. There *could* be someone else, hypothetically. In the capital. Dressing in...onesies...maybe?

Anyway, next we headed to a slightly large warehouse, or was it a shed? Something like that. Did it have cows inside? Was it a barn if it had cows? Terminology, man...

The village head told the kids trailing us to wait outside, and we went in.

"Is that thread?" I asked. When we entered the shed, it looked like the women inside were spinning.

"This is the village's specialty. We process silk thread."

So this world had silkworms too. That was a high-quality material, wasn't it? Did they make clothes with it, then? I looked around; there was something *off*. I couldn't see what, but it made me uncomfortable.

I brooded over it while the village head explained: Apparently the silkworms lived in woods. They carried the cocoons to the village, made the thread, and wove it into cloth and stuff.

Cocoons...?

R-right. The issue was the...cocoons. They were huge. Bigger than a person's head, even. Weird. Maybe something wasn't amiss, exactly, but...

Anyway, the thread and cloth were to be sold to the capital. I looked at the shelves on the wall, where a variety of threads and cloth were displayed.

"Yuna, don't you think this fabric is beautiful?" Shia asked, showing me a light blue fabric.

Cattleya shook her head. "Nothing compared to this, I'd wager."

Cattleya and Shia were downright competing over it now, but they both looked pretty to me. Maricks and Timol looked a little bored, but they still listened in, even if they said nothing.

Maybe I could buy some fabric as a souvenir? Guess I'd ask when we were heading home.

The village head finished his little bout of exposition, and we headed outside.

KUMA
KUMA
KUMA
BEAR

127
The Bear Goes to Save the Villagers

AFTER THE TOUR of the thread workshop, we rejoined the children waiting outside. As we started walking again as a group, I heard someone shouting close by. Then Kumayuru and Kumakyu cried out from Shia and Cattleya's arms.

"Monsters!" someone screamed, and everyone tensed. I immediately used my detection: there were five goblin signals and three other signals farther out.

A crowd gathered. "What happened?"

"Oh, Village Head, I—monsters appeared in the fields!"

"Yes? What kind? How many?"

"Goblins. I spotted three of them myself."

Wrong. Five, plus three more further off.

"Take the men," the village head ordered.

"We'll go as well," Maricks said to the village head.

"No, you students should head inside the house. We can take care of three goblins."

I checked again with my detection skill—there were eight goblins now, and maybe there'd be more soon. Dangerous stuff...

"Shia," I called out softly.

"What is it?"

"There are eight of them now. I'll let you decide. If you want me to, I can go over there."

"No, we'll go."

"But this isn't part of your practical training."

"If you hadn't said anything right now, we would have gone back without doing anything." She shook her head. "I can't do that now."

Shia handed Kumayuru over to me and headed over to Maricks and the others.

"There are more goblins now," she said, "so we're going too."

"Shia?"

"Shia?" Cattleya echoed.

Maricks and the others were taken aback.

"What's wrong, Maricks?" Shia snapped. "Is that sword just for show? Timol, for what other reason do you train with your magic? Cattleya..."

Cattleya nodded briskly. "Don't say another word.

What's the point of having such power if we don't protect the weak?" She handed Kumakyu to me.

Maricks nodded, invigorated. "You're right. Let's go!" he roared, and they rushed after the fighting men of the village. The village head tried to stop them, but the four weren't listening.

Neither was I. What choice did I have? I put down Kumayuru and Kumakyu and chased after them.

When I got there, the goblins and the villagers were squaring off.

Maricks barked instructions, the four spread out, and it was on. Not that it was much to talk about. They were more than capable of dealing with eight goblins. In the end, they worked with the villagers to take 'em out.

Made me feel a bit like a third (fifth?) wheel, to be honest.

As a thank you, the villagers treated us to a real feast of a lunch.

"On this occasion," said the village head, "we'd like to thank you for defeating the monsters. Thanks to you, we avoided any serious harm."

"Do monsters normally appear near the village like that?" I asked.

"No. We have seen them farther out in the woods, but they never come to the village. Monsters aren't fools; they don't encroach on populated territory."

"But you *have* seen them inside the forest?"

"Yes. Increased numbers, in fact. We were all just discussing whether to put out a slaying quest to the adventurers' guild."

As the village head spoke, Timol, Cattleya, and Shia looked over at Maricks for some reason.

Maricks blinked. "What?"

"Nothing," said Timol. "Just that it's you, Maricks, so I thought you'd be like, *I'll go.*"

"Yeah," said Shia, "you'd be like, *leave it to me.*"

Cattleya nodded. "I was convinced you would blurt out that you'd slay them all."

Maricks shrugged. "They're not attacking, you know? The goblins are just chillin' nearby. We're not adventurers here."

Hmm. So the goblins typically settled far away from civilization and didn't mess with populated areas. I was mulling that over as everyone talked and ate when the door flew open.

"Pa!" A man gasped as he barged into the room.

"Garan! What on earth has gotten into you? We've got company, lad!"

"There's no time for that, Pa. Monsters are comin' up near the silkworm nests."

"What did you say?"

"You heard me. I escaped, but Gewn and Geld are still at the shed."

"How many?!"

"More than ten goblins, but I saw more of 'em on my way back to the village. We're looking at twenty, maybe more."

"Goblins again? What is going on?"

"Pa, what do you mean *again*?"

"Goblins appeared near the village just earlier. We defeated them, but..." The village head stood. "More importantly, gather the men! We'll save them all, right away!"

"But most of the men are working. It'll take time for us to gather the...I..."

We were looking at double the number of goblins, maybe more. An average group of guys might not be able to take 'em without truly heavy numbers in their favor.

"Just gather who you can," said Kaboss. "We can talk after."

Well, I *was* the adventurer here, so I supposed I had no choice but to head on over. Or so I thought, but right then? Maricks stood from his chair.

"We'll go save them."

"Maricks?"

Everyone was surprised at that.

"There are people in trouble being attacked by monsters," he said. "Saving them is only natural."

"You just said to leave it to the adventurers, didn't you?"

"Situation's changed. We've got people who can't escape anymore. If we don't go help them this instant, we might not make it in time. What, you want to let villagers die?! And even if they gather reinforcements, we're here right now. We can help till they show up."

Maricks was right. Monsters were attacking them right now, and we didn't know how long anybody would be safe hiding in the shed. I didn't know how many men the village had to gather either, but it would take time for them to prepare.

I had no choice but to go too.

"All of you," I said, "speak up. Because—"

And right when I was going to tell them I had this, Timol spoke.

"I don't mind."

"Cattleya?"

"If their assessment is correct, it's just goblins. It seems there's a larger number, but I think we will manage. Also, if there are lives we can save, we cannot abandon them. What do you think, Shia?"

Shia glanced at me. I stayed silent, pulling my hood

low and keeping mum. Ellelaura had told me to let them do what they wanted, but to save them when they were in danger. I wasn't about to stop them from going out to defeat the monsters. Them thinking and acting on their own was part of the practical training: If Shia and the others said they were going, I'd go with them. If they weren't, I'd go out to help on my own.

"Shia?" Cattleya pressed.

Shia gave me another look to check and turned back toward the others a moment later. "Okay, but with conditions."

"Conditions?"

"First, we don't do anything rash. We stick together. We stop if we don't know for sure that we'll win. And we'll borrow the abilities of Yuna's bears. If we know where the monsters are, it'll be less dangerous, right?"

The three of them thought it over. Finally, Cattleya spoke: "I believe Shia is correct. If we have the bears' detection abilities, it would be less dangerous. It would also make saving the villagers easier."

"Agreed."

"I as well. If we're using the bears' ability, then I'd be fine going. That'll prevent us from being attacked from behind too."

Shia nodded. "Is that also okay with you, Yuna?"

Well, they already knew about Kumayuru and Kumakyu's ability, so why refuse? Besides, Shia probably used that as a pretext to let me accompany them. If they needed Kumayuru and Kumakyu's ability, then the students wouldn't object to my accompanying them, and arguing about it couldn't eat up valuable time.

I nodded. "All right."

With that, everyone stood up from their chairs and started getting ready for the rescue.

"All of you..." The village head was bewildered by the students' actions.

"Sir, may we have someone show us the way?"

The village head looked at the students' faces.

"There isn't time to think it over," said Maricks.

"All right." The village head looked over at the man who had come in earlier—his son, by my guess. "Garan. They're students, but they can do this. Show them the way."

Garan looked the students over for a second before nodding. "Understood. Follow me."

"Please," the old man added, bowing his head, "do not do anything rash."

The students bolted.

The shed we were headed to was partway up the mountainside. We traveled by carriage until we reached the base of the mountains. "We can't go further than this by carriage," said Garan, slowing us to a stop, "so we'll take the rest on foot."

Garan got off and the rest of us followed. Ahead, the path split, and neither road was large enough for our carriage. The shed the villagers were holed up in was up one of those roads, and Garan broke into a run as he led us.

Kumayuru and Kumakyu followed behind on their tiny feet. I used my detection skill too. There were monster signals, though they were scattered. I'd thought there'd only been goblins, but I saw wolf signals too. Kumayuru and Kumakyu would croon when anything got close.

Garan ran ahead on the road. The road was pretty wide, but bumpy.

Two goblin signals up ahead. Kumayuru and Kumakyu let out a little "Cwoon."

"Yuna?!"

"We got monsters."

Garan stopped. Maricks went out ahead.

"From the right!" I called out.

As Maricks and Shia turned toward the right side, two goblins leaped from the woods and were almost immediately taken out without any problem.

"Yuna, are there others?"

"Looks fine, there's none nearby," I said.

We took off toward the shed. We ran wordlessly. I didn't get tired, thanks to my bear shoes, but no one else complained as they ran. Timol seemed like he was having a tough time, but he was still running as fast as he could just behind Maricks.

"Right again," I called out. Maricks and Shia dealt with the goblins, Cattleya and Timol covered them from behind using magic, and that was that.

"Is it still further on?" asked Maricks.

"Just a bit more," Garan called. We were close enough for me to see human signals with my detection...and the monsters surrounding them. The humans were still alive, probably because they were in the shed. Good—we'd made it in time.

Everyone was out of breath except for me. Of course, with my shut-in's stamina, I would've been out of breath as soon as we got into the woods without my bear gear.

They caught their breath for a moment, taking a moment to drink some much needed water.

"Wow, Yuna," Shia marveled. "Aren't you tired?"

"Pssh. Me? I'm an adventurer. I'm trained for this kinda thing," I said, lying. I'd never trained a moment in my life, and no way did I have the discipline to bother trying. But everyone was still looking at me with awe. Even Maricks, believe it or not.

"All right, let's go." Garan took point and started running.

We rushed up a slight incline and there it was: The shed. Along with about ten goblins.

Shia turned to Maricks. "What should we do?"

"We go in fast and hard before they break in. Shia, Cattleya, and I charge 'em. Timol, you track our movements and support us from behind."

"Yep!"

"Yes."

"Mm-hm."

Maricks told Garan and me to hide, then started running off.

As if I was going to listen to him when there might be an emergency. Nah, I ran right after Maricks and the others.

KUMA
KUMA
KUMA
BEAR

128
The Bear Fights the Black Tiger

THE GOBLINS RAINED BLOWS on the shed. It was breaking apart in some places, but it still held, if barely. The goblins were so focused on getting into the shed that they didn't notice Maricks and the others. We were looking at a dozen goblins total.

Maricks, Shia, and Cattleya took down three with their first strike. Needless to say, the other goblins noticed.

Timol blasted flame magic, they scattered—and two of the goblins went right for him.

"Cattleya!" Maricks called. "Cover Timol!"

"If I do that, what about you?"

Right. If Cattleya headed to Timol, Maricks and Shia would have to take on seven goblins by themselves.

"I'll be fine." Timol blasted more magic.

"Shia! Cattleya! We're gonna take them out fast."

"Roger!"

"All right!"

Maricks swung his sword while Shia and Cattleya used their swords and magic to cut down goblins. Just like he'd said, Timol took on the two goblins—but one of them rushed Garan and me.

"Watch out, Miss!" Garan tried to get in front of me, but I lopped off the goblin's head with wind magic. Garan seemed shocked.

Another five goblins appeared, but it was no problem: The surprise attack had worked, and the goblins were as good as dust.

"Is that it?"

"Seems to be."

After Garan confirmed that the goblins were gone, he called out at the shed, "Gewn! Geld!"

Two men came out of the battered shed, bleary and cautious. "That you, Garan?"

"It's okay now. The students from the capital defeated the goblins. We made it in time."

The three hugged each other, happy to be safe.

"You saved us. Thank you," said Gewn to Maricks and the group, the others chiming in with nods.

"But why would goblins appear here?" asked Maricks.

"I don't know. Maybe something happened to their nest?"

The most likely scenario was that they'd run away from adventurers trying to quash them. That, or an even stronger monster had driven them from their den.

While I thought that over, I heard a howl come from deeper in the woods. Kumayuru and Kumakyu practically howled at the sound of it: "Kwoom!"

At that, Shia looked to me. "Yuna?"

I invoked my detection skill, and—

Huh?! That was fast. The signal had barely entered the range of my detection skill, but it was already coming our way at incredible speed.

"Everyone, we're running," I started before catching myself. "No, it's too late to run."

In an instant, dozens of wolves surrounded us, and more by the second. But I could deal with them. Key word being "*I*." But with so many blind spots in the woods, and so many people to protect...

No time to think. The monsters I could sense with my detection were practically flying at us. About to appear, and—

"Everyone, get away from the shed!" I screamed.

"Yuna?" cried Shia, and—

Before our eyes, the entire shed shattered into splinters.

"What was that?!" Maricks shouted.

It slinked out from behind the destroyed shed with deadly grace: a gargantuan tiger with a jet-black pelt.

"Why would something like that be here?" Shia whispered, her voice breaking.

"There's no way," muttered Maricks.

It must've been like a nightmare to them. Unreal. This jet-black beast that was even larger than my bears at full size. It leapt onto the fresh goblin corpses, opened its gaping maw, and dug its razor-sharp fangs right in.

"A black tiger..." Shia whispered.

The black tiger tore into the goblins with its sharp claws, howling with its blood-drenched maw.

We were surrounded by wolves. One bad move and they'd be on us—so many of them now, over a hundred in the rustling shadows. And the black tiger was just too fast. It hadn't even taken a minute to appear after Kumayuru and Kumakyu reacted, and I'd barely seen it on my detection skill before it was here.

"Why's a brute like that in a place like this?" Maricks whispered hoarsely.

No one could answer that question. Everyone could only watch the black tiger as it devoured the feast we'd prepared for it.

"We, um," Maricks stammered. "We need to escape now."

"You can't move," I hissed—the moment Maricks shifted even slightly, the black tiger's nose twitched. It sniffed in our direction.

It was only a matter of time until it decided we were prey.

"Maricks..." Timol whispered.

"What do we do?" Cattleya whimpered.

He was party leader, after all, but, well, it didn't seem fair to count on him right now. He was a student. They all were.

I didn't have a choice. It had to be me.

If I didn't defeat the black tiger and wolves here, there'd be losses at the village. Even if we escaped to the village, we'd bring the black tiger and a hundred wolves with us. There was no telling how many villagers might die. There'd be women and kids who couldn't fight them off... No, it had to be here.

As I tried to explain that, Maricks gulped. Then he looked like he'd decided something. "I-I'll be a decoy," he said with a gulp. "You escape in the meantime."

"Maricks?!" A whole lot of surprised whispers right then. I was just as surprised as everybody else.

"I'm the one who said we'd come here," he said. "This is my responsibility."

"We decided this as a group," said Shia. "It wasn't just you."

Everyone nodded. Maricks winced. "But everyone will die at this rate." The black tiger was still feasting, but it was monitoring its surroundings. If we made a break for it, I think it would've attacked. "I'll buy you some time. Go."

"What if we all ran for it?" asked Cattleya.

Maricks shook his head. "You think that *thing* is going to let us get away?" Everyone looked at the black tiger greedily eating up the goblins. It didn't look good. "Like I said, take Garan and the others. Get out."

Yeah, it was finally my time to step in as an adventurer. I needed to step up to my role as their guard.

And just when I was about to say something, Timol beat me to it.

"I'll stay too, Maricks."

"Timol..."

"I can't just let the girls die. If the two of us are decoys, that should buy us more time. Don't try to get mauled before I do, though."

"Timol, I know you're trying to play it cool, but your hands are shaking."

Not just the hand Timol used to hold his staff, either. He was quivering like jelly all over. "Ha. You should look at yourself, Maricks."

They smiled at each other, but their grins were weak. Friends to the end.

And now I, the girl in a bear onesie, would have to insert myself into this serious scene and totally kill the drama. Oops.

"When we attack, you run. Got that?" Maricks said to Shia and Cattleya.

"Maricks, Timol..." Cattleya bit her lower lip.

Garan and the others didn't know what to do. They couldn't even say anything.

Shia's trembling hand squeezed mine. "Yuna." Shia looked at me, petrified. I turned to her and smiled.

"Timol, let's go," said Maricks.

"R-right." The moment the two moved, I grabbed them by their collars with my bear puppets.

"Wh-what are you doing?!" Maricks stared at me blankly.

"Saving your life, doofus. We're surrounded by more than a hundred wolves. Shia and the others will either end up wolf food or they'll lead 'em back to the village."

Maricks let out a long, defeated sigh. "But then..."

"But then I do my job. Right now."

"What are you saying?"

"The adventurer's taking over. I'm going to save every one of you, got me?"

"But there's no way you can win," he said.

I took a step forward. Maricks grabbed at my bear clothes. I shook him off. "I'll be fine, man."

I reverted Kumayuru and Kumakyu to their original size.

"Kumayuru, Kumakyu, protect everyone."

They replied back with a "kwoom" like they were saying, *Leave it to us*. Other than me and Shia, everyone else was taken aback when they saw my bears at their full size, but there was no time to explain.

"Okay, guys, please keep close to Kumayuru and Kumakyu at all times. You'll be safe if you're with them."

"Yuna..." Shia looked at me worriedly.

"Shia, take care of everyone."

"I will. Please give it everything you have."

I raised my hand in response.

"Shia, you too?" Maricks looked from her to me. "What are you saying? You're letting that bear—"

"Maricks. Trust Yuna here."

"There's no way I can! This was my fault."

"Maricks? Trust. Yuna."

For my part, I entrusted Maricks and the others to Shia and faced off with the black tiger on my own.

The black tiger lifted its massive head from the pile of goblin meat. Turned its great eyes to me. Watched.

It was so much bigger up close, a whole size or two greater than the tigerwolves I'd defeated before, and with a blood-drenched, toothy grin.

Looked butt-ugly, honestly. Should've taken a page from the book of its fellow beasts Kumayuru and Kumakyu and their adorable mugs.

It seemed the black tiger decided I was prey because, in an instant, it howled and leaped at me, instantly closing the gap between us. Its sharp fangs gnashed.

I took a step to the right to evade it.

It was fast.

Quicker than a tigerwolf and more powerful, but I was stronger than I had been back then. Beating it wouldn't be an issue. It'd be over if I lobbed a fire bear, but...

See, that black pelt would've been singed, and where would I be then? I was dying for a nice black tiger-skin rug for my house, preferably not charred. Also, if I used a sword, that'd poke holes in it, and slicing with wind magic would be a mess too. Even ice magic wouldn't do. Guess the right way to go was suffocation through water magic?

So many possibilities. Oh, and I guess I was dodging and exchanging blows and stuff. It was very cool.

As an experiment, I tried restricting its movements with earth magic, but it was too fast to catch. It dodged all the attacks coming from the ground.

Maybe...this? I matched the timing of the black tiger's movements and blew a gust up from the ground with wind magic. The black tiger sensed the force coming from below and leapt up to avoid it, but the wind magic blasted the black tiger into the sky.

Look at that: The big lug was a trendsetter now. He was the world's first cordless bungee jumper.

The black tiger twirled in the air, soaring pretty high up into the sky. It wasn't going to walk away unharmed from that height, but it twisted and strained midair, positioning itself perfectly, landing with the grace of a cat.

You've got to be joking. It came down without a scratch from that height? No broken bones or anything? Ugh.

Right as the black tiger landed, it dashed toward me. I created an earth wall right away to block its path, but the black tiger wove around it. I judged its timing—*there*—and landed a bear punch right between its eyes.

The black tiger flew backward, tumbled, slid across the ground, collided with a tree, and came to a stop... And stood up like nothing had happened. Seemed like it'd rolled with the punch right when I hit.

This thing was stronger than I thought.

Hmm, slaying it while keeping the pelt in pristine condition might be rough. Since it was so fast, I wouldn't be able to pin it down with a golem either. If the Cordless Bungee Strike had at least injured the thing, that would've made it easier.

I was getting a little anxious now. How was I gonna keep my tiger rug nice and clean and perfectly symmetrical?

129
The Bear Slays the Black Tiger

I REALLY DID HAVE to give up. I'd wanted the black pelt pristine, but it looked like I had to resign myself to damaging it a little.

The black tiger was agile, and it had a high aptitude for perceiving magic. It wouldn't let me use the Cordless Bungee Strike a second time, and it could now effortlessly dodge my wind magic like some kinda anime zodiac knight or something—this same-attack-won't-work-twice stuff was *not* what I wanted to deal with right now. It was a *tiger* for crying out loud.

I pulled a sword from my bear storage.

"Dodge this," I muttered.

The black tiger zigzagged forward and came at me with its sharp fangs. I should've dodged, but I didn't think—I blocked instead, and the force of it sent me sliding onto the ground until it was straddling me. It snapped at me with its huge jaws. I kept on blocking. It bit down on the blade with awful, little clicking noises.

I bent my legs and kicked up at the tiger's abdomen with all of my strength. It flew high into the air, spun around and—whoosh!—the cat landed on its feet.

I transferred the sword into my left hand. Had to keep the right hand ready for spellcasting.

The black tiger slowly circled me. Inspecting. This thing hadn't mistaken me for an actual bear, had it? It had to know by now that I wouldn't taste any good, right?

I guess we'd agree to disagree; it closed the distance between us little by little.

The black tiger wasn't landing any fatal blows on me either. Maybe it was getting pissy about it, because I'd heard a low growl rising from its bloody mouth for a while now. It bared its teeth, looking livid.

If I hadn't had my game-breaking bear gear, it'd have been terrifying. With my bear gear and magic, I felt safe, but I could imagine panicking otherwise. As a matter of fact, I wouldn't have been out here to begin with.

The moment the black tiger circled around to my back, it sprung. I hadn't turned around because that would have invited one of the usual attacks. When I turned, its huge maw was trying to chomp through me.

I stabbed at the black tiger's mouth with the sword I held in my white bear puppet on my left hand. The black tiger bit the sword. The moment I pushed the sword forward, it snapped in half.

Crap. It was just a normal iron sword against a black tiger's fangs, after all.

The black tiger assailed me with its razor fangs. I immediately shielded myself with the white bear puppet. The black tiger bit right down.

Ow, ow, ow...ow? Oh. It didn't hurt.

The black tiger drooled as it gnawed on the white bear puppet, but it didn't hurt. Gotta love game-breaking gear.

I forced my white bear puppet down the tiger's throat as it bit me, gathered magic, and launched flame magic into its mouth.

The flame singed the black tiger's throat, lungs, and internal organs—that tiger must've been burning *bright*, but it was all worth it. "Sometimes you have to lose the battle to win the war," after all. Not that I'd...really lost any battles. Or been injured. So...more like "Didn't lose the battle and won the war?" Sure.

The black tiger's jaw loosened, and it leaned over onto me as it collapsed. It wasn't heavy, but it *felt* heavy. I moved the black tiger to the side. It thumped onto the ground.

Neat.

"Yuna!" I heard someone call my name. I looked where the voice was coming from: Shia was rushing over, looking worried. "Yuna, are you okay?"

"It's over. Finally." I'd held back, but that thing had been difficult. Now I had the black pelt, though. I'd have Fina harvest it when I got back.

"I simply cannot believe it," said Cattleya. "You defeated that black tiger by yourself?"

Shia, Cattleya, Maricks, Timol, Garan, and the others joined me. Kumayuru and Kumakyu, who had been their guards, came last. Looked like they'd protected everyone, just like I asked.

"Thanks for doing your job, guys." I gently stroked Kumayuru and Kumakyu's necks.

Everyone else was looking at the dead black tiger on the ground in disbelief.

"Is it really dead?"

"I can't believe it."

"We're not done yet, everyone."

There were wolves everywhere I looked—not just one or two of them either. We were surrounded by more than a hundred. I'd heard wolf howls multiple times while battling the black tiger. They'd probably been calling for friends. I thought the wolves would scram when I defeated the black tiger, but even more had gathered.

"Yuna, the wolves..." Shia gazed at them anxiously. The wolves emerged from the shadows of the trees, one by one...

"There are so many," said Cattleya.

"Kumayuru, Kumakyu, take care of everyone for a little longer."

"Yuna?"

"I have a bit more work to do."

"In that case," said Maricks, "let us help. We can slay wolves."

"You'll get in the way."

"W-we wouldn't..."

"If you get in the way, I'll have Kumayuru and Kumakyu pin you down." At that, my bears crooned and headed toward Maricks. "If he makes a move, just sit on him or something."

And I ran off to face the wolf pack on my own.

Slaying the wolves was a lopsided fight—in my favor, obviously. Landing attacks felt nice. When I fired magic, it hit my mark. As I attacked, the numbers of wolves steadily decreased. I slew the wolves in less time than it had taken to defeat the black tiger.

"And that's that. No more monsters. You can come over now, if you want."

Maricks was looking at me quietly like he wanted to say something.

"What is it?"

"Y-you saved us. Thank you," Maricks choked on his words.

"Yes, you did," said Cattleya. "Thank you very much, Yuna. Thanks to you, we're saved."

"Yuna, thank you very much," said Shia.

"Um, thanks," said Timol finally.

Garan looked around in disbelief. "Um, thank you. Gewn and Geld are safe thanks to you."

"Well, it was my job to protect these kids." I looked them over. Yep, they were fine.

Maricks seemed like he wanted to say something, as per usual, but he kept is mouth firmly shut. He was probably feeling some complex emotions after being saved by me given he'd been convinced I wasn't a real adventurer. He'd even made fun of me. Constantly!

Well, let this be a learning experience—you can't judge a book (bear?) by its cover.

I put the black tiger and wolves away into my bear storage and prepped for the journey back. Well, I called it prep, but we were just cleaning up the goblins Maricks and the others had killed. We made sure to pull off the mana gems as proof of their slaying, too. Shia and the other students were the ones removing the gems, so they could get a little experience.

Also, I may or may not have told them that I was tired and just wanted to watch.

We were going to head back to the village when Garan came over.

"Um, may I request something?" he asked me with some difficulty. "There's a silkworm nest near here. Could we check on it? The nest is very important to the village. Please." Garan bowed deeply.

It was fine, since there were no monsters around, but I couldn't blame him for being anxious after cleaning up a hundred-odd monsters. "It's fine by me, but can you ask the students too? Like I said before, I came here to guard them."

Garan and the others looked at the students, but Maricks was too broody to talk. Shia asked me in Maricks's place, "Yuna, there's nothing dangerous around, right?"

"There isn't. You know I'd protect you if there were."

Shia smiled. "I know. Let's go."

Cattleya and Timol agreed. Finally, Maricks answered with a demure, "All right."

With that, we headed for the silkworm nest.

Since I didn't need to hide them anymore, I rode on Kumayuru. Shia and Cattleya seemed jealous. "What, do you guys wanna ride Kumakyu?"

"Really?"

"May we?"

The two of them happily mounted Kumakyu. Maricks and Timol also watched jealously, but, unfortunately, we were already at capacity.

We got to the silkworm nest with guidance from Garan's group. It seemed this world's silkworms were monsters. Their signals showed up nice and strong on my detection skill.

Then something unexpected appeared right in front of my very eyes: meter-long silkworms wriggling along the ground.

"Thank goodness. They're safe." Garan's group approached them happily. The silkworms were munching away on leaves as though nothing had happened.

I looked around, but I didn't see any damage; they hadn't been attacked. The black tiger either hadn't stopped here or wasn't crazy about eating bugs. Anyway, the silkworms were unscathed.

And nauseating.

I couldn't deal with insect-type monsters, in the game or in real life. Being a shut-in raised in the city, it wasn't like I'd seen bugs too often, so...not a fan. And these bugs were human-sized *and* moving around. Argh, it was almost traumatizing.

Really took me back. See, while I'd been playing the game, there'd been a secret event. It had been called "Let's Exterminate Cockroaches."

When the event started up, it turned the game into a living hell. I logged out the moment I saw 'em and *still* had nightmares for days. Imagine human-sized cockroaches scurrying around. The apex of terror. The event got canceled right away and they distributed items to apologize.

There were some gamers who'd praised the staff for making them look surprisingly realistic, but you *just can't make things like that look real*! It's immoral! Irresponsible! And more importantly, it gave me goosebumps.

Nope. I knew my limit now, and my limit was bugs.

Of course, silkworms moved slower than cockroaches and they didn't attack me, so they wouldn't give me nightmares, but still. Too big. No thanks.

I looked away from the silkworms and took in the cocoons. They were big too. The silkworms were chonkers, so the cocoons were ginormous too. Hooray. I'd solved a mystery that I did *not* want to solve.

Once we confirmed the silkworms were safe, we returned to the village.

130

Maricks Observes the Bear's Fight

"**E**VERYONE, get away from the shed!"

Right as the bear shouted, it appeared—a black tiger, if I remember right. A vicious monster. Why was that thing even here?

I tried to make a break for it, but the bear stopped me. The moment I moved, the black tiger turned its head in my direction.

We couldn't move. If we took even a step, we'd be mauled.

The black tiger was eating goblins. Probably wanted to eat us too, right? Everybody went pale. They were trembling in fear. What were we gonna do? At this rate, we'd be tiger food.

My throat was dry. I took a gulp. Steeled myself. "I-I'll be a decoy. You escape in the meantime."

Then maybe everyone else could escape. Everyone was shocked when I said that. Shia tried to stop me, but at this rate we'd all die. Someone had to stay behind.

"I'll stay too, Maricks."

"Timol..."

"I can't just let the girls die. If the two of us are decoys, that should buy us more time. Don't try to get mauled before I do, though," Timol said shakily. I knew that he was pushing himself to do this, even though he was terrified. I was still happy to hear it.

"Timol, I know you're trying to play it cool, but your hands are shaking."

Mine were too. My hands. We looked at each other and smiled.

We had our minds set. But the second we started running, the bear stopped us. She told us there were more than a hundred wolves surrounding us, so running away wasn't an option. Even if the others could escape, they'd lead the wolves to the village—or maybe even the black tiger.

What else were we supposed to do, huh?!

And in the middle of all that despair, the bear blurted out something so stupid that I had to think it over just to make sure it was real. She said *she* would fight. You know, fight that ferocious black tiger? This girl in a weird outfit? Come on!

It wasn't like I thought *I* could beat it either. I'd be lucky to buy a few minutes for everybody else to get eaten by wolves. But here the bear girl was, going on about how protecting us was her job. This C-Rank in name only expected to what, flash her card at the tiger or something? I couldn't hide my frustration.

But as soon as the bear headed out, I went numb. The little pet bears by her side suddenly grew *massive*.

The hell? We were all surprised—that is, all of us but Shia.

The bear left Shia and her pets to guard us, then started toward the black tiger on her own. She was seriously going to fight it. I reached out to her, but my hand only caught air; I couldn't grab a hold of the bear's clothes.

"Maricks…" Timol said. Even his voice was shaking now. *Shouldn't we be going with her?*

When I tried to go, the black pet bear got in front to block me. Then it let out a "Kwoom…"

I didn't speak bearish, but it was clear enough. The black bear wouldn't let us go.

"What is with you?" I said. "Move over! Your owner's going to get herself killed."

The black bear didn't move.

"Maricks, calm down," said Timol. "If what Yuna said is true, there are wolves nearby. Do you want to attract their attention?"

"Damn."

I looked out at the bear girl.

When she approached the black tiger, it roared and stopped eating the goblins. It bared its fangs. Looked like it would attack at any moment. It was terrifying just to watch. My legs turned to jelly. And in the middle of that fearsome aura, before that nightmarish monster, the bear in the ridiculous outfit walked toward the black tiger. I couldn't do anything. I was powerless.

The fight began. The bear attacked, and the fight turned into something from a dream: The black tiger and the bear squared off as *equals*.

The bear dodged the black tiger's attacks. She blasted magic, and every spell was more powerful than anything I'd seen in my life. And how did she *move* like that? The tiger could barely touch her. She hit. She dodged. They traded blows.

"Shia, did you know?" She must've. Shia was the only one who had reacted differently to the bear since the start. She'd looked at her differently. When I'd told her to take care of that bear, she'd been happy to do it. She *knew* something. "Shia, tell me."

Shia seemed a little hesitant, but she fessed up, "I knew about Yuna from before."

"I knew it. Is that bear really a C-Rank adventurer?"

"She is. Yuna became a C-Rank adventurer on her own merit. She's not some rich wannabe."

I could still hardly believe it, but...I could see it was true. "Do you think she can beat that black tiger?"

Neither of them had injured the other fatally. If anybody was losing their footing, it was the bear.

"I don't know," Shia admitted, "but Yuna is strong. I've heard she slew a hundred goblins, a goblin king, tigerwolves, a black viper, and even destroyed the Zamon bandit clan on her own. I think my mother and father are hiding even more about her."

"Now you're kidding me, though. Right?" I gave her a look. A hundred goblins, a goblin king, tigerwolves, a black viper, and the Zamon bandit clan?

I'd heard about the Zamon bandits from my dad, a knight at the castle. A group of robbers had appeared, targeting the king's birthday celebration. An adventurer had captured part of the group, which let the knights get info on the hideout, and they took 'em out. My dad was part of that operation, of course. He was gone for a couple days.

From what I heard, there weren't many bandits left at the hideout. I heard that their leader had been subdued by an adventurer...and that was *her*?

Plus, a *black viper*? Nah, no way. "That can't be true."

I couldn't believe it. I didn't *want* to believe it. How could that ridiculous girl in a bear outfit be so strong? But there she was, using magic that seemed impossible, doing things that couldn't be real.

Wasn't she scared of the black tiger? We just watched, and this girl—this tiny girl, younger than *me*—fought on all by herself.

"Shia, why didn't you tell us how strong Yuna was?"

"That was part of the test. You can see how Yuna is dressed—that was definitely going to cause issues with you and the others. My job was to make sure that didn't cause any problems, and...well, I didn't want to tell you much."

"That stuff again?"

"In real life, there are things higher ups can and can't say, and they can't just let that get in the way of a mission. This was practice for that—not that you would've believed me if I *did* tell you."

Ugh. She was right—I probably wouldn't have. Wouldn't have thought that some weirdly dressed bear girl was strong, that some girl smaller than me could be stronger. I hadn't even believed her when I learned she was a C-Rank adventurer. I'd just thought of her as another student younger than me, a surprise escort mission at most. I'd told Shia to protect the bear, but she'd been protecting us.

"This is just my guess," Shia said, "but I don't think anyone would believe Yuna was our guard based on how she dressed, even if she really was supposed to be guarding us. Since this is my mother we're talking about, she was probably looking forward to seeing how we'd act." That did seem like Lady Ellelaura. She was right. "But I don't think my mother expected us to encounter a black tiger."

Who *would've* imagined that? And who was going to believe this now? Who'd believe a girl smaller than me and dressed as a bear could take on a black tiger on an equal playing field? Man, I bet I'd get committed if I tried to tell anyone.

I would've been laughing too, if someone told me that. It just didn't seem realistic.

But here the girl in the bear outfit was fighting to save us all. We were all silently watching the bear—no, watching Yuna—and there was nothing I could do.

But Yuna fought on to protect us. She dodged the tiger's sharp claws and pointed fangs, perfectly agile, firing spell after spell with more power than I'd ever seen. What *was* this? How could anyone move that fast, cast magic so quickly and so many times?

Only top-class adventurers could do stuff like that.

Shia wasn't lying. At first I'd intended to fight with her, but I couldn't walk into this without getting in the way. A hot iron taste spread in my mouth; I'd bitten my lip till it bled without realizing.

I was a powerless human.

"Yuna!" Shia cried. The moment I'd looked away, the black tiger was on top of Yuna, its fangs biting into her hand. I moved forward, wanting to help. The moment I stepped forward, Yuna's bear got in way.

"Your owner is in danger!" I yelled, but the bear didn't do anything.

In that instant, Yuna did *something* and the black tiger fell over onto its side. Because I couldn't see around the bear, I didn't know what had happened.

"What's going on?"

"Yuna put her hand inside the black tiger's mouth and fired magic," said Cattleya, voice shaking.

She'd really beat it? The black tiger wasn't moving.

Shia called Yuna's name and started running. Before I knew it, I was running too. I'd never seen an adventurer this powerful, and on top of that, Yuna slew the whole pack of wolves surrounding us, all by herself.

I'd thought I could help Yuna, but she said I'd slow her down. It was upsetting, but maybe it was true. I could only watch her slay the wolves as her bears protected me.

Ten, twenty, thirty. Forty...a hundred...

KUMA
KUMA
KUMA
BEAR

131
The Bear Returns to the Village

AFTER WE CHECKED on the silkworm nest, we headed back to the village. Kumayuru and Kumakyu would've given the villagers a shock if they were still huge, so I cubbified 'em. Maricks and the others were a little startled by that, but they didn't pry.

The village head and several armed villagers stood at the entrance.

"Garan, Geld, Gewn. You're safe?" The village head looked at us expectantly.

"The students and that bear girl saved us," said Garan, nodding at us.

The village head ran right over. "You...you saved people of the village. I can't thank you enough. Words fail me, young heroes."

"Young heroes" apparently did not include bears, because the mayor ran right past me to shake the hands of literally everyone but yours truly for a positively embarrassing amount of time. Look, I didn't *need* the thanks—all in a day's work, etc., etc.—but it still made me feel left out. Maricks really had saved the villagers from the goblins, and I'd just saved the students *with* the whole village and all as a tiny, accidental bonus. Maricks's group deserved the gratitude, but I would've liked *something*. Maybe one handshake? An awkward glance? Anything?

"We didn't really do much," said Maricks, looking from the village head to...me? "The one who defeated them was..."

"Pa," said Garan, "you're not wrong that they saved Gewn and Geld from the goblins, but this bear girl singlehandedly slew a black tiger and—well, about a hundred wolves."

The village head turned from his son to me and back. "A black tiger, you say? A black tiger really appeared?" As if it was too much to believe.

But the others backed Garan up. "I understand if you don't believe it. I hardly can, and I *saw* it, but, it's just as Garan said. This bear girl defeated a ferocious black tiger and over a hundred wolves all on her own."

Everyone looked at me.

"Well, I guess any normal person wouldn't believe that," said Maricks.

"I don't think I would've," added Timol.

"I don't think *anyone* would have," admitted Cattleya.

Rad, cool, thanks...

"But the reality is that Yuna slayed a black tiger."

"Indeed. Yuna defeated the black tiger and the wolves to protect us, without a doubt."

"I still can't believe it even after seeing it, though."

More stares. Agggggghhhrhhhrhgh.

"Then what happened to the black tiger?"

Oh, that was an easy one—I plopped it out of my bear storage. "It's right here."

"This is..." The village head was shocked. "My goodness, it's *massive.*"

There we go. All it took was the testimony of seven-odd people and a monster corpse, and finally he believed me. Truth prevailed.

From there, Garan gave a quick report to confirm the safety of the silkworm nest. "We can thank the students and the bear girl for that too."

"Really, everyone, thank you so very much." The village head gave another round of thanks but (finally) included me in it.

"Thanks," I said lamely. "But I do think you should put

in a quest at the adventurers' guild to check the forest. I only killed the monsters that attacked us."

"Yes, we intend to send a fast horse today."

Then I guess everything would be fine?

Maricks and the others didn't offer to do cleanup, but they were pretty shaken...and the past few days were more than enough proof that they could do the job if they had to.

Once we were done with the report, we rested in our rooms.

"Ahh, I'm beat." Shia flopped on the bed, immediately hugging Kumayuru.

"That is so true," said Cattleya, scooting on her bed to cuddle with Kumakyu. "I shudder to think of what would have happened had Yuna not been there."

Nice to hear, but I still missed my Kumayuru and Kumakyu. I don't know exactly how to put it, but I felt like my hands were weirdly empty. When I saw the two of them petting Kumayuru and Kumakyu, I wanted to get some of that action, too, you know?

"You were so strong, Yuna," said Cattleya.

"No one said I was weak."

"Yes, but...that simply adorable outfit, you know?"

That adorable outfit, yeah. If I were wearing a bear *pelt*

like some cool hunter, people might have thought that was at least a *little* badass. I tried imagining it, but...nope, even with a bear pelt, I couldn't imagine myself with any aura of badass whatsoever. Appearances do matter, huh?

Someone knocked while we were resting, then Maricks whispered from the door. "Can I come in for a moment?"

Once Shia and Cattleya okayed it, Maricks and Timol came into the room.

"What is it?"

"Well, it's...that is, uh..." Maricks looked at his feet. Wait a minute...was this some kinda confession?!

Oh no. Everybody said this happened all the time on field trips, or...I don't know, I'd seen it on the internet. I'd never actually *been* on a field trip before, but supposedly field trips mass-produced couples. Maybe a practical training trip was also something like one of those?!

Were they going to profess their love to Shia? Or was it gonna be Cattleya? Love was in the air, Cupid was fluttering his tiny wings, but *who would be struck*?

I listened closely to Maricks. He said...

"I wanted to apologize before we head out tomorrow."

"Apologize?" Shia repeated, and I could practically see a question mark appear over her head. There was one on top of my head too, though I couldn't see it without un-locking Bear X-Ray vision or something. What was going on? So this *wasn't* a spicy confession? "Do you need to apologize to me?"

"Not you. It's Yuna. I came to apologize to Yuna."

He did *say "Yuna" just now, didn't he?* I wasn't hearing things, right? Up till now I'd been "bear" or "girl," but now I was "Yuna"? It kinda made my skin crawl. Wait, err, back on topic...he was apologizing?

"I talked it over with Timol, and I wanted to apologize before we head out tomorrow."

What was he apologizing for? He'd ignored me and teased me about being a bear, but that was about it? I mean, I was used to that by now, so...

"We didn't believe that Yuna was an adventurer."

What, the girl in the bear onesie, not an adventurer?

"We didn't believe she was strong."

Along with everyone else I'd ever met at first. Even I wouldn't think much of a girl in a bear onesie if I didn't know any better.

"We made fun of you and said you dressed weird."

Okay, true, but I would've made fun of someone dressed so weirdly too. Maricks hadn't really laughed, though. I can't say I'd have done the same.

"We were supposed to listen to the directions of the

adventurer we were traveling with when things got dangerous, but I didn't do that."

They were supposed to *what*? News to me. Well, they hadn't thought I was an adventurer, so what else could they have done?

"Also, I wanted to say thank you to your pet bears." Kumayuru and Kumakyu, who were in Shia and Cattleya's arms, tilted their heads to the side. "Thank you for protecting us."

Kumayuru and Kumakyu had intimidated and driven away the wolves who tried to get close to the group.

"Don't worry about it," I said. "I was the one who was hiding things. Ellelaura asked me to let you do what you wanted. I wouldn't have done anything if things hadn't become dangerous."

"But you were actually protecting us from the shadows, weren't you?"

"It was a job."

"When I thought we'd need to fight a black tiger, I was ready to die," said Timol. "You saved us."

Maricks nodded. "You were the one who had to clean up my mess. I was overconfident thinking I could beat those goblins. Everyone is alive in the end because of you, Yuna."

Err. Okay, all of this yammering about me doing this or doing that was *true* but was also making my back all itchy for some reason. They could stop now. Aaaaany minute.

"Like I said before, don't worry about it," I said quickly. "No one could have predicted the black tiger, and you just acted to save the villagers. Besides, no one would think *I* was an adventurer."

"But..."

"Besides, the two of you didn't really do anything at all. If you'd picked a fight with me, on the other hand, I would've knocked your butts flat before you thought about blinking. So, you know. We're good. Okay?"

Maricks and Timol shifted quietly, looking like they wanted to say something. Shia and Cattleya silently listened in. *I can't stand long silences...*

A knock at the door broke the silence. Shia answered, and the village head's wife entered the room.

"Gracious me, Mr. Maricks and Mr. Timol were here all along? I was wondering where you might have been; I did not see either of you in your room when I visited."

"Sorry, we needed to talk to them about something for a bit," said Maricks.

"We have the meal ready. What would you like to do?"

"That should be fine. Thank you very much," Maricks said, and everyone nodded.

"Then shall we all go?" Cattleya asked.

And we did.

We were treated to the village head's wife's extravagant cooking that night. The village head thanked us over and over again. Then, finally, he said he wanted to thank me in particular, which I...

"No, uh, protecting the students is my job. Don't worry about it."

"But had the black tiger come to the village, I...oh, I simply can't find the words to thank you." Yeah, he wasn't wrong—it would've killed tons of people. "This isn't much of a thank you, but..."

The village head looked at his wife, who headed to the adjacent room and brought back some beautiful cloth and thread. "Please accept this from us," she said with a bow.

"These are...are these from those cocoons?"

"Yes," he said, "from those cocoons. Please make any outfits you like from this cloth."

That, uh, seemed like a pretty roundabout way of telling me that I could stop wearing the bear suit, to be honest.

"Oh, Yuna, I'm jealous!" Shia said as she picked up the cloth.

Cattleya nodded. "These are both high-grade materials."

So this *was* top-notch stuff then. I was a little put off thinking about the massive silkworms they'd came from, but the things themselves weren't bad.

"I had them select the finest goods," said the village head.

"Are you really sure I can have these?"

"My son Garan told me everything. You can't judge a person by their looks. If you hadn't been there, everyone would have died, and terrible things would have come to our village. Please do accept these gifts. They express our gratitude."

"Okay, I slew the black tiger and the wolves, but it wasn't like I really did it to save the village. I was just protecting these kids." I looked at Shia and the students helplessly. I'd just come here as their guard, it was all just—it was an accident, you know?

"Nevertheless, you saved the people of the village. Please." The village head slowly bowed his head. I waited. He didn't raise it.

Yeah, I was just gonna have to agree. "Um, well then, thank you very much."

The village head stopped bowing. He seemed happy.

Between you and me, I'll admit that I did *kinda* want some nice silk after seeing those cocoons. A little bit. And, you know, if he was going to give it to me anyway and wouldn't take no for an answer, then. Well.

Accepting gratitude could be part of the job.

That night, Shia and Cattleya fell asleep the moment they hit the bed. Maricks and Timol were probably out just as quick.

As for Kumayuru and Kumakyu, they spent the night huggled by Shia and Cattleya. I managed to sleep without a fuzzy-wuzzy widdle guy to huggle and snuggle.

For the record, as a professional, I was not bitter in the slightest.

KUMA
KUMA
KUMA
BEAR

132
The Bear Eats Pudding

THE NEXT DAY, the four students still seemed sleepy. Guess they hadn't recovered from their fatigue?

"We loaded the carriage with the goods," the village head explained to Maricks.

I looked to Shia. "Goods?"

"The goods we're going to carry from the village to the capital this time around. I think it's the cloth and thread you got yesterday."

Oh, right. Specialty goods. Hooray.

Once the village head finished talking to Maricks, the old man came over to me. "Ms. Yuna, thank you for everything."

"You already thanked me a lot during the meal yesterday."

"Yes, but…" The village head seemed to hesitate, but he also seemed to realize that there wasn't much left to say. "If you're ever in the area, please stop by. You're always welcome."

The head and villagers saw us off as our carriage departed toward the capital. The carriage jostled us on our way out of the village.

"Still," Cattleya mused, "I never thought we would end up getting into such a mess."

"Sorry about that," said Maricks from the front of the carriage.

"It wasn't really your fault, Maricks. We all decided to save the villagers," Timol said.

"That's right," said Shia.

"You weren't the only one to blame," added Cattleya.

"Um," Maricks mumbled. "Thanks, guys."

The energy was so weird that everyone couldn't help but break out laughing—everyone, from us in the back to everyone up front, Maricks included. Yeah. You know what? This was a good group.

"But, Yuna…you're going to report what happened, aren't you?" Maricks asked.

"Well, that *is* my job."

Cattleya cringed. "Noooo. They'll definitely deduct points."

I shrugged. "There's no avoiding it."

Timol nodded. "That's right. It's essential to know when to give up. I don't think we were wrong in what we did. I don't think going to save the villagers was a mistake either. However, we didn't seek instructions from Yuna, the adventurer, which was wrong on our part."

"I guess so? But at the time we didn't think she was such an amazing adventurer..."

"Shia was also in the wrong!" Maricks groaned. "Weren't you? Keeping quiet and stuff?"

"I told you already, that was part of my test. And thanks to *you* lot, I'm definitely losing tons of points."

Everyone sighed.

"Ugh, fine. Who cares."

"Yeah. The villagers were saved, no one was injured... let's say this was fine."

"All thanks to Yuna."

Hmm. But if I was a teacher, how *would* I grade this?

They hadn't abandoned people in trouble. That was a plus.

They'd put themselves in danger even though they weren't adventurers. That was a minus... Or wait, maybe I should've stopped them before they got into that mess?

But I'd been told to let them do what they wanted if I didn't think it was dangerous. I'd thought it wouldn't be a problem if it was just goblins. I hadn't expected the black tiger or the hundred wolves.

This whole middle management thing was *not* for me.

After that, the carriage kept plowing ahead and we ate bread from the village for lunch. Morin's bread was definitely better though. There was just something different about it. Not that the village was bad, but Morin's bread was something else. After I finished eating, I was left feeling a little unsatisfied, so I pulled out pudding for dessert. *Gotta top off on my sugar.*

I started eating the pudding.

"Yuna, you're eating pudding all alone?" Shia's sharp eyes spotted me.

"You want some too?"

"You'd share?"

I nodded, pulled more pudding out of my bear storage, and handed it to Shia.

"Thank you very much," Shia said and dug in. "Oh, it's delicious."

As Shia and I ate pudding, Cattleya looked at us in shock.

"Y-Yuna, Shia, is...is that..."

"It's pudding. You know what it is?"

I took a spoonful, showed it to Cattleya for a moment, and popped it into my mouth. Delicious.

"Do I know what it is?" Cattleya echoed, shocked. "It was a dish served at the king's birthday celebration banquet..."

Oh, right—I remembered what Noa had said about that business. The hall had gone wild at the banquet when the pudding came out. I'd totally forgotten. "Cattleya, did you attend the banquet?"

"Yes. I still haven't forgotten how moved I was when I ate it." Her eyes welled with tears over, uh. The pudding. "Yuna, why do you have that pudding?"

Hmm. I could hide it, but... Then again, I *was* selling it in Crimonia these days, and people knew it was connected to me because of all the bear decorations. This pudding boat had sailed.

"Yuna made this pudding," Shia answered before I could.

"R-really?! You're...you're the Phantom Chef of the Legendary Pudding?!"

"I...guess?"

Legendary? Phantom *Chef*?

"Did you know about this, Shia? The king would tell no one who made it."

"Yuna treated me to some before the banquet."

Ah, yeah, and we'd chowed down on some pizza together. It hadn't been that long ago, but it felt nostalgic.

Meanwhile, Cattleya kept staring at the pudding I was holding.

"Umm, do you want some too, Cattleya?" I took out a portion for her.

"Are you sure?" Cattleya whispered. "The pudding, I—well, you—but—oh, thank you very much." Cattleya immediately dug in. "Ahh, this is *the* taste. It is so unfair that you've eaten it multiple times, Shia."

"Well, you know what's even more unfair? My sister."

"Whatever do you mean?"

"Anyone in Crimonia can buy pudding at Yuna's shop, so my sister Noa is constantly going there to eat."

True. Noa even snuck out of the house to eat sometimes. Her maid, Lala, was always irritated about that.

"Yuna has a shop?!"

"Yep. Yuna's shop is in Crimonia. On top of that, she sells this pudding at a price even commoners can afford. It's very popular."

"The legendary cuisine served at the king's very own banquet...is being sold at an ordinary shop." Cattleya seemed dumbfounded as she looked at the pudding and me, like I was serving up chunks of the Round Table or something. "A shop? But I thought Yuna was an adventurer."

"Yeah, but I guess you could say I'm the shop's proprietor. I entrusted the management of the store to others."

Every once in a while, I'd come up with a new bread idea and have Morin arrange to make something delicious, but that was pretty much it.

"I see. If I go to Crimonia, I can eat all the pudding I want..."

We had limits in place, so it wasn't exactly a buffet, but...

Shia nodded. "That's why I want to head back to Crimonia soon."

"Oh, when you do that, please do take me with you."

While we girls were chatting, I noticed Maricks and Timol looking our way. Looked like they were interested. Since there was no helping it, I gave them pudding too.

KUMA
KUMA
KUMA
BEAR

133
The Bear Meets Up with Other Students

ONCE AGAIN, I was jostled in the rocky carriage. Things after the village were pretty uneventful; I bet the goblins from before had been chased into our path by the black tiger. No tiger meant no goblins meant a nice, peaceful return trip.

Ugh, if only it had been like this all along. Would've been a real easy job.

Still, it was lonely without Kumayuru and Kumakyu by my side. They were in their cub forms and being carried by Shia and Cattleya, as usual. At least one of them had always been by my side, but now...I was a little lonely. Back in Japan, I never would've cared about stuff like that. I guess Kumayuru and Kumakyu were a little like family now.

Well, that loneliness would end today. Today we were returning to the capital.

The carriage continued at a leisurely pace until Maricks issued instructions for our lunch break. Right at the same time, we found a carriage stopped on the road up ahead. Looked like someone had beat us to the spot; that stopped carriage was also taking a break.

Maricks pointed at the stopped carriage. "Isn't that Jiguldo over there?"

"I'm impressed you could see him, Maricks." Timol squinted ahead, looking uncertain. Shia and Cattleya poked their heads out of their luggage area and looked forward.

"My, it really is."

"Looks like Jiguldo's group."

"People you know?" I asked.

"They're our classmates on the same practical training assignment."

So...more people like Maricks before he got himself together? Great. I thought about hiding in the carriage, but I didn't think that'd fly.

Maricks stopped our carriage behind the other one. The group must've noticed ours, since they were looking our way—two girls and two guys, just like our party. I didn't spot an adventurer guard.

"I was wondering who you were," said Jiguldo, "and who climbs out of that carriage but Maricks and Timol!"

"Jiguldo, are you returning to the capital too?"

"Yeah, but we're a bit behind schedule. You also get held up?"

"Well, you could say that," said Maricks with a smile. Shia and Cattleya headed for the other girls to greet them. Because it would be annoying to explain Kumayuru and Kumakyu, I recalled them before anyone could ask any questions.

"Hey, Maricks. What's with the weird-looking girl?" this Jiguldo jabroni asked Maricks, smiling. Yeah, he was a real Maricks-type, complete with a snotty and infinitely punchable grin.

Maybe I *could* give him a bear punch. That'd be fine, right? Just as long as I didn't do it enough to kill him... right? Yes, I could hear the voice of Bear God telling me as much, deep in my heart: Punch this dork. Hallelujah.

I was just about to start cracking my knuckles when Maricks spoke up. "Jiguldo, bit of advice: If you judge a person by their looks, you'll end up dead. I wouldn't make fun of her, if I were you."

Timol nodded. "Jiguldo, you should work on how you view other people."

Pretty funny to hear all that from *those* two. Shia and Cattleya were practically beaming behind them.

Jiguldo snorted. "What are you even saying?"

"She's an adventurer. Our guard, in fact."

"Your guard? Come on. This pipsqueak little kid?" Jiguldo gave me a baffled look.

"You can think whatever you want," said Maricks, "but don't make fun of Yuna in front of us unless you wanna *answer* to us, feel me?"

Timol nodded at that, followed by Shia and Cattleya a little farther to the back. Getting all mad on my behalf? They shouldn't have. I mean, they *should* have, and I was glad about it, but it would've been nice if they could've been like this from the start.

The guy beside Jiguldo gave Maricks an odd look. "What's gotten into you, man? Why are you protecting that weird girl?"

"Nothing's gotten into me. I just won't let you make fun of our guard, Yuna."

"It's just like what Maricks said," added Timol. "If you make fun of Yuna, you better have bandages ready." Timol and Maricks looked dead serious.

Cattleya cut in—"I would participate as well, of course."

Shia nodded.

"O-okay?" Jiguldo swallowed. "We won't make fun of her, so let's all chill a little." He and his buddies swore up and down they wouldn't make fun of me, so Maricks and the others backed down. Nobody wanted to fight a fellow student.

"But is that girl in the strange—uh, I mean, super adorable bear outfit really your guard?"

"Yeah, she is. She saved our lives. That's why we won't let even you make fun of her."

"Okay, okay! We're all buddies here," said Jiguldo, taking a couple steps back and smiling.

"Seems to be quite the commotion out here. What's going on?" A man and a woman, both adventurers, came out of Jiguldo's carriage. I felt like I'd seen these two somewhere, but I couldn't remember where.

"Jaden," Jiguldo yelled to one of the adventurers. Jaden? I didn't remember any guy named Jaden. Maybe I was mistaken?

"The bloody bear?"

"Huh, is it the bear girl? If I'm not mistaken, it's Yuna, right?"

These two knew about me, but I didn't know them. Maybe they were adventurers from Crimonia? If they were from Crimonia, I guess it'd make sense. Like, I was *kind* of a big deal there. Still, I'd like to have met a person who *didn't* remember me after seeing how I'm dressed. Even if they forgot my face, it was always the bear bit that stuck out.

"Jaden, do you know this strange-looking..." (Maricks scowled at Jiguldo.) "...this cute-looking bear girl?"

"Yeah, she's an adventurer from Crimonia. Every adventurer worth their salt knows Yuna over there."

Yep, I knew it. That's why I remembered seeing them from somewhere. We must've passed by each other somewhere back in the good ol' kraken-slaying days.

"Long time no see, Bear Girl."

I tilted my head to the side. Awfully chummy for a dude I barely remembered.

"What, don't you know me?" asked Jaden, which was pretty gutsy for a background character. No, I couldn't just remember every single face I see in my adventures, my guy. "I suppose that makes sense. We've only talked a little, after all."

We'd *talked* before? Eep. Maybe he was one of the guys I'd punched the first time I went to the guild? But if that was the case, then they wouldn't be so friendly about the greetings.

Processing...processing...no search results found. Ah well.

"Yuna, we spoke in front of the quest board in the Crimonia adventurers' guild. If I remember correctly, it was the day after you made Rank D."

The day I made Rank D...okay, *maaaaaybe* I was starting to remember. A little. "There was a party of four that I spoke to when I was looking at the C-Rank board, right?"

And try as I might, that was about all I could recall. Not their names, not their faces, just a nondescript four-person party of men and women before taking the tigerwolf quest and going with Fina to slay some monsters.

"So...you finally remember?" asked the woman. The word *remembered* was doing a lot of work here. Did this... count as remembering? "I'm Mel. He's Jaden. Nice to meet you."

"What about the other two?" It was a four-person party back then, after all.

"They're guarding other students. You're a guard too?"

"I am."

"Jaden, is that strange..." Jiguldo coughed loudly. "... that is, very cute and wonderful bear girl that I'd never ever insult...really an adventurer?"

"She's made a name for herself through all kinds of things," said Mel. Pretty vague, but there *were* a lot of things, eh?

"You're all taking a break too, right?" asked Jaden. "How about joining us?"

It was a fine idea. Maricks's group gave the horses food and water, then we prepared our own meals.

"Still," said Mel, "I had no idea you were taking jobs at the capital."

"I happened to get a quest from an acquaintance. I hadn't intended to accept it, but she wouldn't take no for an answer." If Shia wasn't there, I might've weaseled out of it...

"You should be thankful to her. This quest is easy with a high payout, so it's popular."

"Is it?" I'd heard there weren't enough people. Had Ellelaura tricked me? But then, she said she'd just been *selective*, so maybe it wasn't a lie?

"All you're doing is escorting the students to a nearby village. There aren't any dangerous monsters around the capital, so it's a piece of cake."

Eh he he. Was it, now? We all put on strained smiles. There was no way they'd believe us if we said we'd encountered and slain a black tiger.

"The students don't do anything dangerous, it's an easy job," said Jaden with a smile. I glanced back at my four party members. The boys looked away. The girls smiled.

"Jaden," said a girl from the other group, "is that girl dressed as a bear really an adventurer? She looks like she's younger than us." At least she was being more polite than Maricks had been.

"It's true," said Jaden. "She's a stronger adventurer than me."

Jiguldo's party was astonished at those words. I couldn't blame them. I didn't want to hear this right now either.

"I can't believe it." The girl looked at me. She wasn't wrong, you know? If people had to place bets on a fight between Jaden and me, no one would bet on me. It'd seem like way too much of a longshot.

"Right. Everyone who sees her says that," Jaden answered with a smile, "but she's stronger than she looks, and she's a highly respected adventurer."

"Jaden, do you know a lot about Yuna?" Shia asked.

"Just the rumors."

"What kind of rumors?"

The conversation was heading in a strange direction. Even though this was supposed to be a break, I got the sense it would head somewhere dangerous if I didn't stop it here. It was time for my secret technique...

"Rumors aside, more importantly, what are you guys doing in the capital, Jaden?" I asked, using my forbidden power of "changing the subject"!

"As a rule, we work in the capital. We just happened to hear a rumor when we were doing a job in Crimonia."

"What kind of rumor?" Oh no. I could see it, now: We were back to the original topic.

"There was this bear girl who came to the guild to

register as an adventurer. She beat all of the D-Rank and E-Rank adventurers who picked a fight with her into bloody pulps."

It wasn't *all* of them! The only person I bloodied up was Deboranay. I dropped everyone else with one punch each.

"She bloodied them up?" The students looked over at me. Since I had done it to Deboranay, I couldn't say it was a *lie*. But it'd only been one person.

"Yuna, you're amazing." Shia was delighted.

"Nah, they were just weak."

"So, what other stories are there?"

They were going to keep going with this? Couldn't they stop now? Surely Shia had heard enough from Cliff and Ellelaura.

"She slew a goblin king, for one."

"A goblin king?!"

"Yeah, its face was frozen in this brutal, angry look. It was something else." (Well, I *had* dropped it in a hole and unleashed a one-sided massacre upon it, so guess that would've made it angry.) "We happened to be at the adventurers' guild when we saw it. I can't believe you had the gumption to fight such a brutal monster."

So Mel and the others had seen that, huh?

As the students listened to the story, their expressions

were evenly divided. Maricks's party did believe it. Jiguldo's party did not. Polar opposites.

"But that's not what really made Yuna famous in town. No, that was—"

"The black viper?" Timol finished. "I heard about it from Shia, but is it really true?"

Thinking about it now, it was a fishy story. If I hadn't brought the viper's body back, I don't think anyone would've believed me.

"We didn't actually see it either, but many adventurers believe it."

"Why is that?"

"A black viper was attacking a village. A child from the village came to Crimonia crying for help, but no adventurers at the guild could defeat one. We were at the capital at the time, but even if we'd been there, I'm not sure we would've accepted the quest."

"So what happened?"

"Bear girl accepted it like it was nothin'. She didn't even negotiate the fee. Just went off to slay it by herself because the village was in trouble. The adventurers didn't think she could take it. Made fun of her something nasty—this wasn't some goblin king. The size and power of a black viper are on a completely different level. All those adventurers thought the bear girl was a goner."

Was that true? Then again, I'd immediately rushed out of the guild with the kid, so I hadn't paid much attention.

"But get this: Several days later, she returned with the corpse," said Jaden.

"They didn't talk like that anymore—not with the proof lying dead in front of them," added Mel.

Just listening was embarrassing.

"I don't believe it," Jiguldo insisted, understandably.

"Believe it or not, but all the adventurers in Crimonia know what they saw," Jaden said, and he looked at me. "No one in Crimonia's said a nasty word about the bear girl since. They all know what's up."

Even with Jaden's explanation, Jiguldo's party seemed to think it was made up. But Mel went on: "There's been even more gossip recently..."

"Oh, really?" Jaden shook his head. "One every day, I swear."

Mel just laughed. If it was recent, did they mean the kraken? Or maybe the tunnel? Both of them would've sounded fishy.

"What is it?" asked Jaden. "What's the rumor?"

"They say she beat a kraken. Boiled the thing up and served it on silver platters."

"You're pulling my leg. A *kraken*?"

Kraken it was, then. The two of them laughed. Everyone looked at me.

"Yeah, c'mon. A kraken is, uh." I twisted my lip. "That's just, uh. Nah. Me? A...kraken?"

Finally, after a few more embarrassing folk tales from Jaden, our break time came to an end.

KUMA
KUMA
KUMA
BEAR

134
The Bear Returns to the Capital

WE GOT BACK to the capital without a hitch, and the practical training came to a close. Soon, I'd return to Crimonia and sleep in my own bed for the first time in a billion years. You just can't get a good night's sleep in a carriage or camping out, you know? You've gotta get back to your own home.

Of course, I could also rest easy knowing that Kumayuru and Kumakyu were present and available for cuddles, but that was obviously just a tiny little fringe benefit.

We passed through the gate and the carriage headed toward the academy. I held my guild card up to the crystal panel and the nearby soldiers gave me a weird look, but there weren't any issues getting into the capital.

At the academy, there were already some carriages at

the parking area behind the school building. Seemed the other student groups were already back.

"That's that, huh?" I hopped down from the carriage and took a nice, long stretch. Got the kinks outta my spine, all that good stuff. The deed was done. There'd been a bit of trouble (army of wolves, etc.) but the students had come out unscathed. Another S-Rank mission accomplished.

"Yuna, we have to report our return to the teacher."

Blargh. I was on duty until the report. Ah well. Almost there.

"Jiguldo! You guys are going too, right?"

"Yeah, we're going. Wait up a bit."

Oh—and when we'd met up with Jiguldo's party on the way, we'd ended up traveling together. We'd been headed in the same direction, after all, and more people meant that monsters would have a harder time dealing with us. Even if bandits showed up, they were less likely to try anything if they were outnumbered.

We headed to the staff room of the school building to meet up with the teachers and met someone unexpected.

"Pardon us."

"Mother!" Shia shouted out to Ellelaura, who was standing beside her teacher. "Why are you here?"

"I instructed the gate guard to promptly contact me upon your return. I categorized the order under S-Rank business, so the report came fast." She smiled broadly, as if that was a sound explanation instead of kinda sorta probably an abuse of power. "Thank you, by the way, for your work."

Whew. Feel bad for the guy who ran all the way from the gate to the castle to tell Ellelaura.

The teacher nodded absently. "Maricks and Jiguldo's parties have completed their practical training. We'll take care of the goods you transported here, so feel free to rest. I'll take your training report on a later day, but no fibbing, you hear me? I'll be comparing what you have to say with the reports from your accompanying adventurers."

The students seemed fine with that. Maricks and the others were free to go home, but—hold on, did that mean I wasn't off the hook yet?

"Yuna, thank you very much for this," said Shia. "It was fun being with you."

"It was a bit of a pain," I said, "but...I had fun too."

"Yuna," said Cattleya, "please give Kumayuru and Kumakyu my thanks. Please let us cuddle with them again next time." She seemed sad. At one point she'd even asked me to let her have my bears, but I'd politely declined. I couldn't just give them away. Kumayuru and Kumakyu were my dear family. Priceless.

"Yuna," said Maricks, "I'm going to train more and become a knight who can protect others like you."

Not a knight, Maricks? An adventurer? Hello?

"I feel like I learned a valuable lesson from this," said Timol, bowing his head. "Thank you very much."

"Oh my," said Ellelaura, "they're all such polite kids."

But the teacher looked puzzled. "What's going on here?" I didn't have an answer. I mean, I hadn't known exactly what they were like before. He'd have to figure out their character development himself.

The students left the staff room together, leaving only Jaden and Mel and me. It was time to give our reports. A pain, but it was part of the job.

"Well then," said Ellelaura to the teacher, "I'll take her report over *there*, hmm?"

"Lady Ellelaura, I don't see why you need to do that... do you?"

"Oh goodness, it's no trouble. I just want to hear what she has to say, and you need to talk to the *other* adventurers, don't you?" Ellelaura looked at Jaden and Mel.

"I see...I...I'll leave the young lady bear over there to you."

Good to hear. Thinking about it now, I didn't want to

tell the teacher about that black tiger. Ellelaura, on the other hand, already knew me.

And here I parted with Jaden and Mel.

"Yuna, we'll come to Crimonia another time," said Mel. "When we do, let's do a job or something together."

"We could even go slay a dragon," I responded to Mel's lip service, which made her and Jaden laugh.

Ellelaura and I stepped away from the teacher and took a seat. "Good work, Yuna. How was it?"

"Exhausting. I didn't think I would be this tired traveling by carriage." Another reason I was glad to have Kumayuru and Kumakyu most of the time.

"Ha! Thank you, Yuna. Wasn't it a good experience?"

What, was it supposed to be an *experience*? I don't know, it had certainly been...linear events. I gave Ellelaura the report on the practical training. Told her about the goblins, about Maricks and the others, about the village and the black tiger. I'm sure Maricks's group would confess the whole thing so I couldn't hide it.

"A black tiger..." Ellelaura looked shocked.

"Don't go too hard on the kids. They just tried to save the villagers. We didn't know there *was* a black tiger, and I didn't stop them."

"I suppose no one could have done anything about it. Don't blame yourself. I'm afraid to think of what would have happened had you *not* been there."

If I hadn't been there—I don't know, maybe it could've gone all right. I suppose with the wrong adventurer guarding them, though, they might've wound up dead. "Are they gonna lose points for it?" Sure, it had been dangerous, but they *had* gone to rescue those villagers. That had to count for something.

"From a tactical perspective, they would lose points, but... Yes, I think that was better than abandoning people. Those children are the future of this country. If young aristocrats abandoned their fellows easily, well... Then again, if saving people is truly impossible, it's important to give up. I think the children have learned an important lesson."

So had they lost points or gained them? Or had Ellelaura herself not decided yet?

Hmm. Everybody had their own way of thinking, and figuring out right from wrong was hard. If they lost points, maybe they wouldn't help people next time. If they got praise, maybe they would do something rash again. Education's tricky.

"I must thank you for what you did, Yuna. Thank you for protecting the children."

"It's fine, that was the job, but I'm turning you down next time."

"That's too bad." (Didn't seem too bad for me, but okay.) "Well then, what's your opinion of everyone?"

"Maricks can make decisions, but he can only see what's immediately in front of him." Which had its pros and cons.

And Timol? "Timol is timid, but when push comes to shove, he toughens up." When Maricks chose to stay behind and take on the black tiger, Timol tried to do the same.

Cattleya? "She can really read a situation."

And Shia? "I think you'd know her better than me." Besides, Shia had known about me from the start, so it was hard to be neutral with her.

Ellelaura asked me a few questions then, which I answered. Before long, the report was also over, and I could finally go home.

But when I stood up, Ellelaura called out to stop me, "Yuna, wait a minute. Here, take this."

Ellelaura gave me a thin book she retrieved from her item bag. There was a bear illustration on the cover. It was that picture book, *The Bear and the Girl*, that I had drawn for Lady Flora.

"The picture book is printed. I thought I'd give you a copy."

I flipped through the pages of the book. It was nicely bound, actually. Kinda made me feel good.

"Hmm?" Oh, weird—as I paged through the picture book, something piqued my interest. "*The Bear and the Girl,* with story and art by...'Bear'?"

Ellelaura nodded. "It's better than having your real name on it, isn't it?" She wasn't wrong, but something about "Bear" seemed odd. "Of course, we *can* print your actual name the next time we bind your books, if you wish."

"It's fine, Bear is good." As long as it wasn't my name, why not? I could just think of Bear as a pen name... And a pretty fitting one, admittedly.

"You just wanted ten copies of each, right?" Ellelaura pulled more picture books out of her item bag and set them on the desk. Ten each, including the copy of the first in my hands. "The books are all the rage. Delighted reviews all around. You could sell them countrywide."

"I have no plans for that." If they spread across the country, there'd be pressure for another volume, and another volume, and another... Nah, it wouldn't be fun if I was forced to work on it.

"Well, let me know if you want to sell them. We can go big whenever you'd like."

"I have to politely decline."

"Oh, that's unfortunate. Lady Flora and I *are* looking forward to its continuation though. What do you think of *The Bear and Ellelaura* for the next title?"

"Why would your name be in there?"

"You're the bear, aren't you? In that case, why couldn't I appear with you?"

"If I did make another one, it'd be with Noa. If you made an appearance, you'd be the villain deceiving the bear."

"Oh goodness, me? Deceptive? How terrible. Though I'll admit, I would like a picture book with my daughter in it."

"I'm not going to draw any for a while though." I needed a break...

"So you *will* draw it *after* a while, hmm? Then please, you must make sure that Noa and I are *exceedingly* adorable in your illustrations."

I ignored Ellelaura and put the picture book into bear storage. I'd give them to the orphanage later. These would help the kids study their letters a little.

This time Ellelaura really *was* done, and I headed home. I'd been thinking of saying bye to Jaden and Mel, but the two of them were already gone; there was no way they'd have more stuff to report than me, so they'd probably finished earlier. I headed out of the academy on my own.

I guess I had bad timing, though, since I ended up joining in with the students heading home.

"Isn't that the bear from the other day?"

"That's the rumored bear."

"So cute!"

"There's a bear walking around?"

"Wonder where they sell clothes like that?"

"What's up with her and Ellelaura?"

"I want to give her a hug."

They had the same sort of reactions as when I'd come by the academy before.

Right when I was about to make a break from them all, Maricks and the others appeared in front of me and glared at all the gossiping students.

Huh. Didn't see that coming. "What is it, Shia? Weren't you headed home?"

"We were waiting for you."

"Why?"

"We wanted to thank you, of course." Shia grasped onto my bear puppet.

"You saved our lives," said Timol.

Cattleya nodded. "We talked together and decided to thank you."

"Yuna, let's grab something to eat."

"Since we're students, we don't have that much money, but we know a place that's cheap and tasty."

But the sun was close to setting... "Is it okay if you all stay out? It's already late."

"It's fine. Our families still don't know that we're back."

Then wouldn't it be bad if they didn't get home soon?

Nope—Ellelaura knew they were here.

"It's normal to have a party after the practical," said Shia.

Cattleya nodded again. "We're heading out, Yuna."

Shia and Cattleya pulled me along. Maricks and Timol followed behind us. There was no escape.

The students treated me to dinner.

Yeah... It was good.

KUMA
KUMA
KUMA
BEAR

135
The Bear Heads to the Orphanage to Deliver the Book

IT WAS EVENING on the same day the students bought me a meal. After getting back to Crimonia, I collapsed onto my bed in my white bear outfit, post-bath and ready for nappin' in the comfort of my own home.

What would I do without my bear transport gate? Probably die instantly.

Yeah, sleeping in your own bed really couldn't be beat.

I summoned my bears in their cub form. Shia and Cattleya had been hogging the bears for a while, and I really missed their fluffiness. Like huggable melatonin or something, they were so comfy that I was gonna be out in a millisecond. My eyelids started to steadily droop.

"Kumayuru, Kumakyu, I'm going to bed now."

I fell asleep, sandwiched by my fuzzy little buddies on either side, and slipped into a dream.

When I woke the next day, I found my bears sleeping curled up on either side of me like cinnamon rolls by my pillow. I gently stroked and then recalled them.

I changed into my black bear outfit and headed out to the Bear's Lounge for breakfast. The smell of freshly baked bread wafted over to me at the back entrance; Morin was baking inside. The kids were working their darndest to knead the bread and make pudding around her.

"Yuna, you're back?" Morin called out, and the kids looked over at me too. Morin warned the kids when they tried to approach me: "I know you're happy to see Yuna come here, but we need to prep for opening—wait till then before your breaks, all right?"

I nodded, putting my bear puppets on my hips for good measure. "Everyone, listen to Morin and get your work done first."

"We wiiill!" they practically sang. Morin rolled her eyes a little but couldn't hide her smile.

"Morin, can I have some bread?" Eating oven-fresh bread was a special privilege that came with owning the place, but I also needed to order up some bread to replenish the supply in my bear storage. I was running pretty low after the practical training mission.

"You can take whatever bread you like."

Oh, you *know* I was gonna wreck that fresh bread. A delicious aroma wafted over me. I didn't know which to choose. Truly, this was the worst situation anyone could ever be in.

I brooded over the decision, and the kids watched me. Maybe some of the bread had been baked by them?

I picked out a couple of loaves and watched them immediately divide into a delighted group and a disappointed one. *Sorry, guys.*

Maybe I could make my way through all of their bread someday.

I went for the refrigerator to get juice, but Karin just brought some over for me, smiling.

"Thanks." I took a big swig.

"You're welcome. You sure are popular with the kids."

Popular? Maybe. It felt more like they were chicks attached to me because I'd fed them. I picked at my bread and watched them work. "How's the shop?"

"We're super busy every day, like usual."

"Do you have enough people?"

"We're fine on that front. Mil and the others do a thorough job of things."

Hmm. Suddenly I felt a little guilty that I was the one putting those kids to work. I mean, it *was* normal for kids to work in this world, mind you. Kids on a farm helped out with the farming, merchant's kids helped out with the business. There were a lot of cases where kids would help out with their parents' jobs at a young age. It was pretty normal.

That even applied to Karin here. She'd been baking since she was young. "They're such dedicated workers." She flashed a strained smile. "Much better than I was at their age."

"You didn't help out?"

"This girl," someone called out, "was always goofing off."

"Mom!"

Morin cackled. "In fact, this particular problem child wouldn't help at all, no matter how many times I asked her to."

Karin rubbed her eyes. "Moooooom..."

"Oh, don't give me that. It was only a few years ago, mm?" Even though it seemed like old news to Karin, it was apparently fresh in Morin's mind.

"You didn't help out, Karin?" the kids looked at Karin with their innocent eyes.

"Of course I did. I just skipped out a teeny-tiny bit." She was wiggling her hands now as she talked. It was kind of adorable.

Morin nodded absently. "A teeny bit, mm?"

"*Mom*!"

"Ha, I'm kidding. You're earning your keep now, dear."

"It's not like I'm still a little kid."

"Yes, of course not. You've grown so much. Father would be proud of you. I'm sure he is."

"Oh, Mom, I..."

As mother and daughter shared a touching moment, the kids started forcing their way in.

"I-I'm being really thorough about learning too."

"Me too..."

"And me."

The kids started to advocate for themselves.

"Oh my, look at all these apprentices. Karin, if you become too complacent, these kids'll start overtaking you."

Karin laughed. "All right, the lot of you. Let's get back to work. I'll race you, eh?"

The kids ran after her. Morin watched their backs in delight.

Yeah. It was good to be back.

Once I finished eating breakfast, I headed to the orphanage to pass out picture books. The bear ornament was there to greet me. It was supposed to be a guardian deity to protect the orphanage, but it looked more like a cartoon mascot than a fearsome protector.

I passed by the bear and headed inside. The shop gang was hard at work and the kokekko gang was in the henhouse. I realized the only ones around would be the little kid gang—some little guys ranging from about five to six. Even the five- and six-year-olds helped the headmistress take care of the smaller kids—by playing with them, admittedly, which probably wasn't that much labor-wise.

The little kid gang was in their playroom. I actually found the headmistress and the smaller kids there too.

"Headmistress, good morning."

"I see you're back from your job, Yuna."

Like hounds called to a hunt, the little kid gang ran over to me on their stumpy legs and latched on.

I gave them head pats and squeezed my way to the headmistress. "Yep. I came by to see how the kids are doing and bring them some souvenirs."

"A soo-veh-near? Wassat?" one of the kids holding my bear hands asked.

"Is it food?"

"Is it *yummy* food?"

"Sorry, it's not edible."

"Aww..." Maybe I should've picked up snacks instead?

The headmistress shook her head. "You must not say such selfish things. Thanks to Yuna, we're able to eat delicious meals every day."

It wasn't really like it was thanks to me. No, it was the older gang of kids working at the shop, taking care of the kokekko, and putting food on the table. All I did was set up the foundation. Everyone else had done the hard work.

"Yes, ma'am, we're sowwy." The kids apologized.

"I'll bring some yummy things for you next time, okay? The souvenir I've got for you today is a picture book."

"A pik-chur book?"

I pulled out *The Bear and the Girl* from my bear storage.

"It's a bear!" One of the kids took the book from my hands.

"Aw, no fair. I wanna see too!"

"But I wanna see..."

"Don't fight over it." I pulled out another volume of the book. "Make sure you all share it when you read it."

"We wiiill!"

The kids started to read the book together.

"Yuna, thank you so much," said the headmistress.

"There's also a second volume, so please read this one to them when they're done." I handed the headmistress two copies of the *The Bear and the Girl*, Volume 2.

"Oh my, what charming illustrations."

"If you'd like other picture books, please let Tiermina know."

"It should be fine. Those kids won't be selfish."

"And picture books will help them learn to read. Nothing selfish about that."

"Oh, marvelous! Come, everyone, make sure to thank Yuna."

The kids looked up at me from the picture book they were reading and thanked me.

"Everyone, make sure to study really hard. Don't cause any trouble for the headmistress."

The kids agreed with great enthusiasm. After that, I spent my time talking to the headmistress about what had happened recently, and I finally read the book to the kids.

136
The Bear Spots Anz

A FEW DAYS AFTER I got back from the capital, I was just loafing around. You know, stuff like popping into the adventurers' guild; taking Fina, Shuri, Noa, and my bears for walks; visiting the bears at the honey tree; just really enjoying this fantasy world.

So there I was, lying around on my bed with my bears since morning. You *could* call it lazy.

But I didn't have anything to do, or anything I wanted to do. Every once in a while, when I ended up with free time like this, I was dying to have the internet and my video games back. This world was fun, sure, but it wasn't a great place for hobbies, ya know? Hmm... Maybe I could get the orphans together and try setting up an old board game with them. Othello, shogi, chess, snakes and ladders, playing cards... I could've come up with more, too, if my stomach hadn't suddenly groaned.

Oops, forgot about eating again. I'd been lounging around on my bed all day without even eating breakfast. I decided to head over to the Bear's Lounge to fix that.

On my way to the shop, a familiar face came my way.

"What? You're headed out?"

Cliff, my dude, you don't even have a guard! It seemed aristocrats thought they could get away without body-guards in this world. Noa slipped out and walked around the town on her own all the time too. The king had even dropped by my house once, though I think that one must've been a one-off. No way any regular king would waltz around on his own, in this world or any other.

Was Cliff really so safe or was he just way reckless? I *hoped* it was the former. The local guards checked for felons at the gate, after all, and I saw them doing patrols all the time, so maybe the streets really were safe.

Although, in the fantasy worlds from books and games and stuff, aristocrats and their daughters always had loads of guards. The daughters especially. And the guards would be mega-handsome, and then the daughter would fall into a sweeping forbidden love with one.

Noa, despite being the daughter of an aristocrat, didn't have a handsome guard like that. I supposed giving a young lady some hot guy to follow her around might cause weird rumors and mess up the whole feudalism marriageability thing.

Granted, if Noa had appeared in a manga or novel, she probably would've lived a life surrounded by hot guys.

"I'm hungry," I said to Cliff, shaking myself out of my hot guard analysis, "so I'm headed out to eat. What about you, Cliff?"

"I was on my way to your house."

"My house?" Weird. Sure, Noa came by a lot, but Cliff rarely dropped by for home visits. I mostly got messages from him through their family maid Lala or from Noa herself.

"I had something I wanted to discuss with you. I'm feeling a bit peckish too, actually—may I join you?"

"I don't really mind." And I wasn't going to say no to an aristocrat either.

Cliff and I headed to the Bear's Lounge together, just a slight distance away from my bear house.

There wasn't much of a reaction from anyone in the shop. Nobody gave us unpleasant looks or anything. If I'd been in the capital, on the other hand, it'd be all "A bear's come in here!" followed by a commotion and staring and the word "bear" and probably at least one hijink. In this shop though, I heard nothing of the sort.

I came here to eat in my bear outfit all the time. Everybody knew this was my shop, and my outfit fit in with the kids in their bear jackets—kids that were milling around the place right then, matter of fact.

Cliff and I headed to the counter. A girl in a bear jacket greeted us. "What'll it be, ma'am?"

Uhh, good question. Everything looked good. Eventually, I ordered two hamburgers (which were Morin's new items), a serving of fries, and juice. Cliff just asked for the same as me.

As a rule, I paid whenever I came through the front as a customer. That was why I started to pull out money, but Cliff wouldn't have it—this was on him.

"Are you sure?"

"Don't worry about it."

After picking up our order, we took a seat—me on one side, Cliff on the other.

"So, what did you need from me?" I picked at my fries.

"It's not something I need from you so much as something I need to tell you. The tunnel improvements should be completed in a few days."

"Cool. It's about time." I nommed down on one of Morin's new hamburgers.

So the lord of the land himself had come all this way to tell me the tunnel was done.

"We didn't *have* to modify it, but we needed carriages to be able to fit inside. We needed lights, too, a rest stop for the horses, and some prep for the surrounding roads. It took quite a while," Cliff explained as he ate his fries.

Fair enough. That was why I'd left further tunnel stuff to the experts. This wasn't something a layperson like me should butt in on. I'd rubber-stamp whatever as long as I had my secure stream of seafood.

"So people from here will be able to get to Mileela then? It won't be a problem?"

"We were already bringing them flour and other necessities, but now people without a formal connection to the town will be able to go through the tunnel. From here forth, part of the toll will be transferred to your guild card, as per our agreement. If you want to know more, you can ask Milaine."

Cliff and Milaine had brought a contract to my house a while ago. It had been too much of a pain to read it carefully, but I remembered that it said the tolls would be delivered to my guild card and I'd be able to use the tunnel for free. That applied to the people who traveled the tunnel with me too.

"Did you get some inns set up?"

"Two so far, though that may not be enough. Regardless, Mileela's mayor and the trade guild will handle that. I told them to let me know if they didn't have enough people. It should be fine."

We really wouldn't know how things would turn out until the tunnel was open. How many people would travel for trade, ocean viewing, work, or leisure? If there were a ton, two inns wouldn't be enough to board them all. On the other hand, if only a few people used the tunnel, we were set.

Oh, if the tunnel was done, did this mean I'd see Anz soon? I'd asked Tiermina to help out with Anz, but the two of them didn't know each other. Considering I'd finished up my work at the capital, it would be perfect timing to bring her over.

"Well, this shop's cuisine is delicious," Cliff said with a smile. Always nice to hear a positive review from a fancy aristocrat, eh? Then again, I'd secretly been feeding the bread to the king without telling Morin. This was officially royalty-approved product. It *had* to be good.

After I'd given Morin a vague description of what I knew about making Japanese breads, she'd used her own stores of knowledge and experience to pull off the recipes—and she was still doing research to make new varieties.

This was probably the best bakery in the kingdom!

Wait, nobody would try to poach my baker or anything right? Maybe I needed to give Morin a raise, just in case...

"Well, I have work left to do, so I'm heading back. If you need to ask about anything, come by the estate."

Cliff ordered some bread before he left—possibly as a treat for Noa.

A few days after I heard about the tunnel stuff from Cliff, there was a formal announcement of the project's completion.

Most people knew about the tunnel. Given the tree clearing, the roadwork, and the monster slaying, it wasn't hard to put things together. Needless to say, the townspeople didn't seem very surprised. They were happy, in fact.

A few more days passed and while I was walking around town, there was a slight commotion.

Had something happened? I didn't have anything better to do, so I headed over and found a ton of carriages stopped at the town's gate. All around, the crowd was talking about Mileela. The carriages came in one after another, carrying people from the seaport. A man who looked like a merchant was consulting with the gate guard about all kinds of things.

Where can we park the carriages?

Where is the trade guild?

Which inn do you recommend?

The guard courteously answered each question.

As I watched, people started leaving their carriages. Turned out they'd been packed in pretty tightly, as an absolute ton of them poured out. Among them was a familiar-looking lady who still, after all this time, didn't look remotely related to Deigha Kong.

That was definitely Anz. I hadn't expected her to come as soon as the tunnel was done. Four women stood next to her. Probably the ones she'd told me about.

They were looking around the place, seeming like total country girls out of their element. I headed over, trying to keep them from noticing me. My bear shoes were silent enough for the stealth approach.

But nope, Anz whipped around and looked right at me.

"Ms. Yuna!" Anz cried giddily, running over to me. I'd been hoping to surprise her, but I'd flubbed it. What gave me away?

"I'm surprised you noticed me."

"I mean, if everyone nearby is saying, 'There's a bear here,' 'There's a bear,' then I think it's a, ah, fair assumption."

Yeah, the people from Mileela and Crimonia *were* all looking at me. Ugh, this bear gear was totally unbalanced. Even if no one could hear my footsteps, my appearance was a dead giveaway.

"Ms. Yuna, you didn't come out to welcome us, did you?"

We'd arranged to meet at the orphanage. "Nah, just a coincidence. I was just walking around and saw the commotion. But I thought the tunnel was just opened? I didn't think you'd come this soon."

"There were so many carriage reservations to Crimonia that we weren't able to get one at first, but the trade guild reached out to give us priority."

"Oh yeah?"

"Yes! It's Jeremo's way of showing his appreciation. In exchange, he told us to talk Mileela up around here. As for my job, I look forward to it: Let me assure you that I *will* earn my keep!" Anz beamed at me.

She sure was cute. Flash that smile at a guy instead and I bet that'd get Deigha a son-in-law real quick. She was cute and could cook perfectly—honestly, I couldn't figure out why she was still single. Didn't have a boyfriend, that was.

Probably Deigha's fault. He'd asked me to get Anz a fiancé... Maybe that would go a lot quicker without him around?

"Well, Crimonia's so big! I feel like I might get lost." Anz looked over the town. It really was a lot larger than Mileela, and more populated too.

As we talked, the women behind Anz gave us a look. One of them tugged on Anz's clothes. "Anz, you haven't forgotten us, have you?"

"Won't you introduce us to the little teddy girl?"

The other women nodded along. Wait...what teddy?

"Oh, sorry. Ms. Yuna, these are the women I told you about the other day. They'll help with the shop."

Right, so these *were* the four women I'd heard about. They were between twenty and twenty-five years old...if they hadn't just aged crazy well like Ellelaura.

"Can we call you Yuna? Or maybe Ms. Yuna is better, since we'll be in your care from now on?"

"You can call me anything you'd like *except* for 'Teddy,'" I said, looking at the woman who'd called me that. Her hair was tied up behind her head.

"Aww, but I think Teddy is so cute."

Cute? It made me feel like a stuffed animal, or maybe a scraggly little bear cub! Nope, I didn't like it. "Under my authority as a small businesswoman, I forbid it."

"A small businessteddy...?" (I glared at her.) "Uh, all right. Then we can call you Yuna?"

I nodded. If anyone heard her calling me by my real name, others might copy her. I could deal with "Bear Girl." I'd made a little life with Bear Girl. But *Teddy*? Nope. I had to put my footie pajama down on Teddy.

"In that case, I'll call you Yuna too."

They each introduced themselves. The oldest looking one was Neaf. She was lovely and had a magnanimous smile. The youngest (and the "Teddy" criminal) was Seno. She looked to be about twenty. Then there was Forne. She kind of gave off older sister vibes for Anz and Seno. Lastly, there was Bettle. Her hair was meticulously trimmed and she looked like she meant business.

"Are you sure you're all right with all of this?" asked Neaf. "We're not bothering you, are we?"

"Nah, not at all. I think Anz likely already told you, but you're lifesavers. I don't know anyone who can prep seafood." There were rivers around here, but no ocean and no ingredients to learn with.

"The job is just to prep fish and cook?"

"Mainly that, yeah, though it'd be a lot of work for Anz if she had to stock and manage ingredients and manage the money." There might be other things they'd need to do too. I'd been thinking of asking Tiermina to help out, but she was busy. All of this was a little bit my fault, so I wanted Anz and the others to manage the shop as much as they could on their own.

"Anz, we're counting on you to teach us."

Anz blushed. "All of this is a first to me, too, though."

I shook my head. "We at least have someone who knows a lot about stocking up on ingredients and managing money, so you can consult her at the start." Okay, I'd asked Tiermina for a *little* help as we got started here. She knew the most about where to get veggies and stuff and how to balance books as well. "Anyway, let's talk business tomorrow. You must all be tired from your ride on the carriage, right?"

"Um, Ms. Yuna, could you recommend an inexpensive inn to us?"

"An inn?"

"I think we'll need to get an inn quickly or other people will snatch up the rooms. We'll just stay there for now, then we can find a place to live tomorrow."

"You don't need to do that. You can live above the shop; it's pretty spacious."

"Above the store?"

"Yeah, it'd probably make opening up shop easier, right?" They'd have a zero-minute commute. It was excellent real estate—going between the shop and home was easy, and they'd be able to rest right away if they got tired from work. "You can use the shop's ingredients for your meals, so the lodging and basic board is free. Anyway, you can talk it over together and figure out what you'd like to do."

Mostly I just wanted to get away from the crowd. The looks I'd been getting nonstop since my arrival were starting to hurt. In particular, there were a lot of eyes on me from the Mileelans. It'd be a pain if any of them tried to start up a conversation, so I took Anz's group and left.

137
The Bear Shows Anz Around

Anz's group ogled the town like they'd never seen anything like it before. I'd done the same thing when I got to Crimonia for the first time, so I wasn't one to talk, but I'd been looking around to figure out whether I was in the game world or in an alternate universe...and all the while, everyone had been looking at *me,* this interdimensional bear onesie girl. At least the locals didn't do that anymore.

Somehow, it'd been a few months since I'd arrived in this world... *Man, tempus really do be fugit.*

The women talked among themselves:

"There are so many people."

"Yeah, for real."

"Are we really working in this town?"

"I wonder if I can manage it."

"Well, we've got each other!"

"All the townspeople are dressed so nicely."

"Yeah, but...I don't see any."

"You're right."

Just as I was wondering what they didn't see, they all turned to look at me. Uhh? "What do you not see?"

"People wearing outfits like yours, Yuna."

"There aren't any other bears."

"We thought that there would be people wearing bear clothes in town like you."

All of them nodded.

But...*huh*? C'mon, no way townsfolk would walk around town wearing a onesie like me. This had been a onesie-less world till I showed up.

Then again, if a person lived in Mileela all their life *and* hadn't gone anywhere else before *and* hadn't heard anything about Crimonia, I guess they'd assume people in town might wear onesies if the first Crimonian local they'd ever seen was me?

Then again, there were people heading to Mileela from Crimonia to work, so my outfit still had to have seemed a little weird.

"So no one else wears clothes like you, Ms. Yuna?"

They were really going to make me answer that one out loud, huh? "Um. Ah. No."

That was the only answer I could give. What else could I say? I couldn't hide behind the kids working at the shop with their outfits. After all, those were just jackets. Parkas made to look like bears—like the ones on the kids coming up to us right then.

My eyes landed on a crowd of 'em walking around. They were definitely the kids working at the Bear's Lounge. Wh-what were they doing walking around in a place like this? Actually, why were they walking around wearing the shop uniforms?

And at a time like now... What was going on at the shop? The gears in my mind spun at maximum power, but they weren't spitting out any answers.

While I tried to get a read on the kids, Seno noticed them. "Huh?! There *are* bears. Those kids are dressed up as bears."

At that, everyone looked toward the kids in the bear jackets. The kids noticed me too.

"Yuna!" The kids scrambled over to me—three girls.

"What are you all doing in a place like this?" I asked. "What's happening with the shop?"

"We have the day off."

Ohhh, right, today was their weekly free day. I hadn't visited the shop, so I'd forgotten.

"Ms. Yuna, who are these kids?" Anz asked.

Even if I tried to wave it off, she'd find out eventually, so I gave her an honest explanation. "Oh, they're my orphan workers." Then I turned to them. "But why are you all wearing your uniforms? The shop really is closed today, right?"

"Well, because it's cute and warm," one girl answered with a full and honest smile.

"Also, Tiermina said that we'd be safe as long as we wear these."

"You'd be safe?"

"She said we'd have the bear's protection, so we won't get caught up in anything bad or get tricked. We wear them when we go out shopping."

"Oooh! And when we go shopping? We get free stuff!"

When they said they got the bear's protection, did they mean...I was the bear? Because being dressed as a bear only ever seemed to bring *me* fights.

Were they really going to be okay? I'd need to check in with Tiermina on her logic. What if they got bullied? "So why are you all here?"

"We came to buy ingredients. Headmistress asked."

"Yeah! We got the day off, but everybody else is working."

Agh, too cute! "You're all so good." I gave each of them a head pat. They squinted happily. "Be careful while you're out shopping, guys."

It wasn't like I could waste their time too long while they were on errands. They were all thumbs-up and enthusiastic nods as they left.

"They're such cute kids, aren't they?" Neaf cooed. The others agreed—they were so well-behaved, so sweet.

I nodded. "The headmistress who looks after them is a nice person. The kids follow her example, so they've grown up to be really good."

Good really was the word, huh? The orphans had grown into upstanding kids thanks to the headmistress and Liz.

After we left the shopping kids, I started walking to the shop where Anz's group would be working. Then something caught their eyes.

"Huh? What's that?"

"A bear?"

"Looks like."

"Is that a shop?"

Everyone was looking at the Bear's Lounge. Anz's shop was nearby, so of course they would see it as we headed there.

A giant bear stood in front of the entrance. Other bears decorated the rooftop. A sign read Bear's Lounge in big letters. They all stared at the shop and bears, their mouths agape.

"I've...seen something like this before."

"Oh, what a coincidence. Me too."

"Me as well."

All of them nodded, then looked at me.

"It's the same as the bear in front of the tunnel, isn't it?"

Ding ding ding, we've got a winner.

"That one was carrying a sword, but this one has a loaf of bread."

"How cute."

"Yuna, this isn't your shop, is it?"

Sigh. "It's one of the places I manage."

"Then were the kids we just saw employees from here?"

"So that's why they were dressed like bears."

"We're not working here, too, are we?"

They all had a different expression—worry, anxiety, a forced smile, and delight.

"This shop mainly sells bread and light meals. I've prepped a different shop for you."

"You did?"

"Since I'm planning on having the new shop focus on rice and seafood." You just *had* to have rice with fish, after all. Then again, we didn't have rice right now, or even miso, so...I guess we'd only have seafood for a while?

"Actually, what's been going on with the Land of Wa?"

"One of their ships came the other day to start trading." Finally. Maybe soon I could get my hands on rice, soy sauce, and miso... "Jeremo said that he would send you the things you requested once he got them."

I was looking forward to it. Looked like Japanese food might soon reenter my culinary life!

I took Anz and the others toward the shop. Well, I didn't really have to take them far since, as noted, Anz's shop was close to the Bear's Lounge.

Once we got there, the group stared in awe at the giant building in front of them.

"It's huge."

It was smaller all around than the Bear's Lounge, but it was still two stories and on the large side generally speaking.

"But there are no bears." Seno placed a hand to her forehead and searched the surroundings.

Well, the only reason why we'd ended up with bears on the outside of the shop in the first place was because Milaine had made the uniforms, and I'd had to elaborate a little on that.

"Let's make bears for this shop too," said Seno, looking to Anz. "You want bear decorations too, don't you?"

"I don't mind either way."

"Then why not? Since it's Yuna's shop, I'm sure that people from Mileela will just like it all the more."

Forne nodded. "True, true."

"Oh, and let's make the bear unique. It could hold a fish."

"What if we gave it rice too?"

Seno nodded sagely. "You're right. That would be a good way of getting word out to people in Crimonia too."

"Anyway," I said through gritted teeth, "let's talk about that *later* and go *inside*. I'm sure you're all tired."

"Of course," said Seno from behind me, "one statue is the bear minimum, and..."

Yeah, Seno had taken a liking to the bear decorations.

Well, it wasn't like I'd fight putting up decorations if they asked. I'd already given up on that front. Trying to resist didn't do anything.

Then again, this time, maybe I'd put up a teeny-tiny bit of a struggle.

Once we got inside the building, a huge, open space spread out before us. This was the dining area.

"Sure is empty, isn't it?"

"But it's so large..."

Anz and the others started walking through the room.

"Are you sure we can open a shop in here?"

I nodded. "Yeah, it'll be yours, Anz."

"Wow."

"Hey, as long as you like it, it's whatever."

"Yuna, can we head to the back?"

After I gave my okay, Seno and the others started exploring the first floor. It had the kitchen and storage. Since it'd originally been a normal house, it had baths and stuff too. Anz and Neaf headed to the kitchen. Seno and the others headed to the storage and bath areas.

"This is nicer than the one in our inn," said Anz from the kitchen. Wasn't too surprising, since we'd cleaned the area up. Tiermina had done most of the work.

"The bath is nice too," said Seno, and suddenly cried out excitedly: "And ohmigosh there are even bears in there!"

Everyone rushed to the bath.

"That's a bear right there."

"Yeah, it's a bear all right."

"It sure is a bear."

Just like the bear house, the hot water came out of a bear's mouth. Look, don't ask me... The bath had needed some repairs, so I'd rebuilt it.

"But this sure is large."

"Yeah, I think all of us could fit in here."

"Though it might be hard to clean."

All true. "Be sure to talk with each other about keeping it tidy while you're using it."

After she'd mostly examined the first floor, Anz headed up to the second floor. The second floor was the living quarters.

"There are five rooms here, so you can use the ones you like," I said.

Seno opened a door nearby and gasped. "Yuna, you don't mean this room is for a single person?"

Since I'd heard that Anz was going to have four helpers, I'd furnished each room with a single bed. If they brought on more people, then they would need to share rooms, but right now since there were five of them, Anz included, they could each have their own.

Seno shook her head. "I never would have thought we'd each get our own room."

"Well, we were all thinking of renting a house," said Anz. "We wouldn't have been able to get separate rooms if we wanted an inexpensive place."

"Yuna, we are going to get wages, right?" Seno asked me anxiously. Come to think of it, we hadn't discussed pay. I needed to consult Tiermina first.

"I'm going to pay you properly. It's just that I need to ask the person in charge of finances to figure out how much."

"Okay, I'm fine even if it's a small amount, as long as we're paid something."

"If we get to live in a place like this, we really can't complain either way."

Yeah, I'd talk with Tiermina tomorrow. "Also, this is going to be a women-only house, so make sure you don't bring any men here. If you want to fool around with boys, please do it somewhere else." Since they were young women at a particular age, things like that might happen, and—you know, whatever. Just as long as they weren't bringing strangers into the house.

"I'm good as far as men go for the time being."

"Same here."

"My husband was killed, so I'm sure you can figure out the rest."

All of them except for Anz nodded. Some of them had lost their husbands and children, after all, so the rule might have been unnecessary. Maybe I should've spoken more carefully. "Is there anything else you want to know?"

Everyone looked at each other and shook their heads slightly. No questions right now, looked like.

"All right then, rest up for now."

It was already night. There wasn't time to show them around town, and I was sure they were tired from the long trip. I wanted them to rest early.

I laid out some bread Morin and the kids had made on the table for them to have as dinner and breakfast. "Well, I'll be back tomorrow morning, so take it easy until then."

After that, I stopped by Tiermina's place real quick and headed home.

138
The Bear Explains to Anz

IT WAS THE DAY AFTER Anz had come to Crimonia. While I was waiting at home, Tiermina came by. "Morning, Yuna. Am I a little late?"

"Right on time. I'm counting on you today." There were a lot of things I needed to talk to Tiermina about when it came to the shop-slash-living-area that I'd given to Anz and the others, so I'd asked her to stop by. I knew she was busy in the mornings, but Tiermina had still agreed. "But you're sure you'll be okay?" I asked. "Work won't pile up?"

"It should be fine. My daughters went to help out in my stead, and Liz is there too. It might take them a while, but they'll make sure to get everything done. Don't worry."

Liz had apparently been managing the eggs and dropping by the trade guild. Tiermina had taught Liz how to fill in for her, knowing she might get sick again at some point in the future. Still, Tiermina had been taking care of things for me this whole time, and I was going to rely on her again now...

I took Tiermina to Anz's shop. When we got inside, Anz and the others were hanging around the first floor.

"Oh, Ms. Yuna. Good morning," Anz greeted me.

"Yuna, morning." Neaf also came by and greeted me.

"Morning. You guys sleep well?"

"Yeah, we got to sleep. The beds were so fluffy and felt so comfortable." Anz didn't look tired at all—yeah, she'd gotten some good rest.

"Yuna, are you really sure we can use those rooms?"

"And for free?"

"Even though you're paying us?"

I guess they'd really liked the rooms. They were all dubious.

"You're not getting us involved in any funny business, are you?" Seno added.

Their eyes all centered on me.

"I'm going to pay you an actual wage for really normal business." Though I could see how it might seem too good to be true. Of course they'd feel anxious. I didn't know much about how the workforce in this world was normally treated. I'd happened to hear that apprentices were sometimes provisioned with necessities without a real wage, though that probably depended on the type of work.

"So, Ms. Yuna, who's this?" Anz asked about Tiermina, who stood beside me.

I introduced Tiermina to everyone, explaining that she was the mother of Fina and Shuri, who these women had met in the past. I also told them she'd be helping with the shop, focusing on the finance work. With that done, I introduced the group, Anz included, to Tiermina.

"Sorry for imposing on you, but we are looking forward to working with you!"

Tiermina smiled. "If there's anything you don't know, you can ask me anything."

"Yes, ma'am! Thank you."

Once Anz and the others had finished introducing themselves, we moved to a break room on the first floor and started talking next steps. "I'm going to give a simplified explanation of the work. Ready? If you have any questions, just chime in."

From there, I gave them a concise summary about my vision for the shop. Anz would be responsible for management; everyone would follow her directions, it being her shop and all. Anz would design the menu and decide what dishes to offer—though they could discuss it with each other, Anz had final say. The others would help out with the shop and the orphanage. After every six days of work, they'd get one day off, just like at the Bear's Lounge.

"I'm going to be responsible for things..." Anz murmured.

"Tiermina and I are going to help you, so don't worry." *Especially Tiermina*, I added internally. I wondered if she could sense that somehow. Her smile looked pretty... was strained the right word? I'd maybe say *anticipatory* instead.

"Well," said one of the women, "Anz just needs to cook like Deigha."

"Okay, I'll do what I can." Anz nodded diminutively.

"Anz, when you make the menu, please make sure to write out how much of each ingredient you need. We'll discuss stocking costs and price points for selling once you've done that."

"Yes, I will," Anz answered, looking earnest.

"Also—and we won't do this for a while, but—you should decide on how many of each item we'll sell in a given time frame. If we don't figure that out, it'll cause issues with our stockpile."

"Of course. We would have a problem if we bought too much and the ingredients spoiled."

"Will you be procuring the ingredients, Tiermina?"

"For now, at least. Of course, once you've gotten to know the town and have a little more time, you can start handling it on your own."

"All right. In that case, I'd like to see the ingredients in person. Could you tell me which shops they come from?"

"Yep," said Tiermina. "I have some butchers and grocers to recommend. I'll show them to you later."

"Thank you so much!"

"What about our work?" Seno asked, raising her hand slightly.

"You'll learn how to cook the food from Anz and support her. You'll total sales, manage the ingredients, clean the shop—and I suppose also look after the orphans?" Hmm. Anything else?

"So mainly we're helping out Anz?"

"Yeah, just don't let her work pile up."

"Of course we won't. We're here in Crimonia because Anz agreed to bring us. We won't cause trouble for her."

"Thank you, everyone," said Anz cheerfully. She looked over at the older women, a determined look in her eyes. "I'm going give this everything I've got."

From there, Tiermina explained their wages and such. I mean, I had no idea what a fair rate would be. All I'd told Tiermina was to pay above average—no way did I want any headhunters coming for my people.

It seemed Tiermina did that part well, because she got no complaints. In fact, they asked if we were really okay with paying so much! Apparently, you usually deducted money from a person's wages when they lived on site, but I'd told Tiermina not to.

"Are we really okay with this?" I asked. "Anz, don't regret saying that."

"Wh-why would you say something so frightening?"

"Because the culinary skills you've developed under your father are far greater than you believe. Don't undersell yourself."

I wasn't kidding. We were probably gonna get swamped after people tasted her food. At least, that's what I hoped. There was always a chance the shop would flop. But Deigha's food, and Anz's by extension, *was* delicious. It'd probably be fine, as long as word of mouth spread fast enough.

"My dad's cooking is great, but my skills are still in development..."

"The food you cooked up was crazy good, Anz. C'mon, puff out your chest a little. Have some pride."

"Th-thank you. I'm going to give it my all."

"But we're not about to bump your wages up for a day just because things are hectic for a while."

"I-I understand."

Everyone laughed, which was good because that was a lie on my part. I was planning to increase their pay as we sold more. I needed Anz to save up a good amount for her dowry, after all. Regardless of what kind of guy she got hitched to, having money wouldn't be a problem, even if it led her to quit her job someday.

Next up—interior design!

"As you can see, stuff's pretty barren right now. Why don't you guys decide what you want?" The inside of the shop was empty. The chairs and the table in the break room we were using had been there from the start, but they weren't the kinds of furniture you'd use for a shop.

Anz blinked. "We get to decide?"

"It's your shop, Anz. Make it how you want. Once you've decided, just put in a word with Tiermina and she'll place an order with the furniture store. Or maybe the carpenters? I don't know, it'll be some kinda merchant."

Tiermina sighed. "I knew I'd be the one doing it."

Anz winced.

I smiled sheepishly. "Aaaanyway, if there are any tools or whatever you want for the kitchen, make sure to mention that too."

"Oh! I brought over my tools from home, but I don't have enough for everyone. I suppose we'll need more."

"Then just look into what you need. You can also tell me what plates and cups you'd like to use for serving the food."

"Um, I can really choose the plates and such?"

"Yeah. But make sure you talk to Tiermina about cost."

"Yes, Yuna!"

From there, we decided that Anz would devise the menu and split up the jobs in the next few days.

With the shop out of the way, we covered the orphanage next. I explained that the orphans were taking care of kokekko and working at the Bear's Lounge—the kids in the bear clothes, I clarified.

Neaf interjected at that point. "Yuna, what did you want us to do for the work at the orphanage? Should we help the kids take care of the birds?"

"The kids have got that covered, so I'd like you to look after the littler kids and do other chores. I'm sure the kids'll help out, too, but if you could do things like the laundry, cleaning, and cooking? There are so many kids that they're really having a heck of a time. Oh, and if you have time, I'd like you to give them some early lessons on reading, writing, and arithmetic."

The kids used their free time to study, at least, but the headmistress wasn't able to manage the education of every single one of them on her own. If the kids couldn't read or write, they might get swindled by a contract someday. If they couldn't do math, they *also* might get swindled in the future. No matter where the kids went, they'd need these skills both to protect themselves and give them a wider range of opportunity.

"That seems unexpectedly hectic," said Neaf. (Well, yeah—the headmistress and Liz were doing the work on their own right now. It was a handful for sure.) "Yes, with kids, you have no idea what they're thinking or what mischief they'll get up to." She laughed softly. Her eyes were distant. "It's an awful lot of trouble to take care of them."

As though she had experience... Oh.

Some people who'd been saved from the bandits had lost their children. Neaf might have been one of those people. I wasn't going to ask her, but...

We finished talking and headed to the orphanage to introduce the group to the kids.

139
The Bear Leads Anz and the Others to the Orphanage Part One

AFTER WE FINISHED the explanations, I led Anz and the others to the orphanage.

"Tiermina," said Anz, "you're Fina and Shuri's mother, aren't you?"

"Yes. And I heard that they were treated very well in Mileela. Thank you."

"Oh," said Anz with a wave of her hand, "we just made them food."

"*Delicious* food, I'm told."

"Not compared to my dad's."

I shook my head. "Nah. Your cooking's delicious, too, Anz."

"Ms. Yuna..." Anz seemed delighted. It wasn't like I

was giving her empty flattery either. Anz's cooking really was fantastic.

"Ha! Well then, Anz, I'm looking forward to your cooking too."

"Um! Then...then I'll give it everything I've got."

While we were talking, we caught sight of the orphanage...and of *that*.

"Another tiny bear?"

"It's a bear all right."

"This bear is cute too."

The kids had requested a bear statue in front of their newly built orphanage, so there it stood.

Seno beamed. "We should definitely make bear decorations for the shop too."

Tiermina nodded. "It's Yuna's shop, so it really is a requirement."

Yep, I'd have to make a bear statue for Anz's shop, too, if this kept up.

Must...resist... Maybe Anz could help me? "The shop belongs to Anz, so it'd be weird for there to be a bear there, right? Don't you think, Anz?"

Come on, Anz. Come through for the bear girl here!

"I wouldn't mind having a bear..." she said, turning her eyes away.

Anz had betrayed me.

"So you think so too?" If vipers could smile, they'd look a little like Tiermina there. Seemed Milaine was influencing her. Maybe they'd hit it off without me noticing?

"In that case," said Seno, "I think we've got to have the bear hold a fish."

"Fish are a given, but maybe a squid or octopus might be nice?"

"In that case we need one with shellfish too."

Tiermina nodded. "Why don't we make them all?"

Hold on, what did she mean *we*? I'd be the one making them! Just like when Cliff forced me to make the bear statue in front of the tunnel... All of these schemes were branching out from Seno. And here I was without allies—with Anz and Tiermina both turning against me. Despair... Agony... Horror...

"That's enough about the bear decorations. Let's get inside." Pretty please? We were at the door, and they kept talking!

I took them in and headed to the kids' playroom. We found them gathered around the headmistress for a picture book reading.

"Welcome, Ms. Yuna."

"Morning, Headmistress."

The kids who noticed me came running up.

"Bear girl!"

The kids latched onto my stomach, legs, and arms. If I weren't wearing my bear gear, they probably would've toppled me right over. Even a large adult might've been knocked down if three or four kids glomped them.

I guess my bear gear was working as usual, since I wasn't knocked over by the kids grabbing onto me. The room was all smiles. That included Neaf—though her smile looked a little forced.

"What brings you here today?" The headmistress looked at Anz and the others behind me. "And who might these people be?"

I briefly introduced everyone. I explained that they'd come from Mileela and would be managing a shop in Crimonia.

She nodded. "Right, and these are the ladies who will be doing that." I'd told the headmistress earlier, and that I'd like to have the kids work there just like they had at Morin's bakery. Of course, I didn't want to force any of the kids or the new arrivals into any of this stuff, but I wanted to offer everybody options.

This applied to Anz, too, but there was no telling whether she'd stay forever. She might get married or move back to Mileela. I was hoping she'd teach the kids how to do the job before then.

"I'm Anz. It's nice to meet you." Seno, Forne, Bettle, and Neaf introduced themselves in kind.

The headmistress nodded. "Greetings! I am Bo. I take care of these kids at the orphanage. I've heard about you all. You'll work at Ms. Yuna's shop then? It will likely be a lot, but I hope you do well."

"So, Headmistress...uh, I was thinking of having everyone help out at the orphanage too?"

"At the orphanage, you say?" The headmistress seemed a little surprised.

I'd told her about the arrivals working at the shop, but not about the orphanage. I'd wanted to get Neaf and the others to agree to it first—you know, so I didn't put anybody on the spot. "It's my fault that you and Liz are having a rough time. I even asked Liz to take care of the kokekko."

"Oh, dear, thank you for thinking of us, but we're fine. The kids are all good and, most importantly, you and Tiermina have helped us. I don't believe we're in a tight spot at all. We had trouble finding food to eat before we met you. We no longer have to worry about that, and now I can spend more time with the children." The headmistress stroked the head of the kid on her lap.

Sure, she was saying all that, but I could tell she was having a rough time. A different kind of rough from before we met, but still rough. The only things Tiermina and I were doing were giving jobs to the kids. It wasn't like we were helping take care of them.

"I don't know, Headmistress, I mean, what if you collapse or something?"

The kids looked horrified. "Headmistwess, are you gonna cowwapse?"

The moment I floated that, the kids ran over to her seat, grabbed at her clothes, and latched onto her arms— all looking worried that at any moment, the headmistress might explode into dust.

"I'm fine, dears. I won't collapse." Even with them holding onto her, she didn't so much as totter. She might've been stronger than me even without the bear clothes on.

Still, she seemed troubled as she stroked the kids' heads and placated them, even if it was a really adorable image.

"Please make sure you don't collapse for the kids' sake, Headmistress. I'll help you so that won't happen."

"Ms. Yuna, thank you."

Now that I had approval from the headmistress, I led

Anz's group over to the kids who were taking care of the birds.

I headed by the fence where the kokekko were, next to the orphanage.

"We keep 'em fenced in to stop the birds from wandering off," I told them.

Inside, the kids were catching the birds and shutting them away in the pen. The kokekko had been multiplying a lot recently, so they'd partitioned the henhouse and were cleaning it.

"Once we get the birds into the pen," said Liz, "we're having lunch."

"Okaaay!"

Liz was putting the birds into the pen with the kids when they all noticed us. "Ms. Yuna? And Ms. Tiermina?" Liz looked at us with a kokekko still in her hand. "Ms. Tiermina, I thought you were busy today?"

"This is that business I mentioned earlier."

"Ah, right."

"Did the egg deal go all right?" Tiermina asked. Liz had gone to sell the eggs today.

"Yes, it went fine. I made sure to double-check our count before I handed them off at the guild."

"Thank you."

"Oh, it was nothing. Fina helped too."

"Where are my daughters, by the way?"

"They're working inside the pen." While we were talking to Liz, the kids gathered around us. "I know you're happy Yuna's here, but if you don't hurry, we're going to be late for lunch."

Liz told the kids to go back to work. After I told them to "go get 'em" the kids nodded and headed back to their job.

Liz smiled. "Everyone becomes so motivated whenever Ms. Yuna comes by."

"They're all taking their work seriously, aren't they?" said Seno.

Anz nodded. "It seems like they all like you, Ms. Yuna. The kids with the headmistress ran over to you as soon as you came into the room."

I shrugged. "It's because I look like a bear."

"Oh, Yuna, you know very well it's not that. The kids are always so happy when you come here. They even work harder," Tiermina said with a smile.

Liz nodded. "Even the troublemakers take things seriously when you show up."

Okay, fine. I wasn't about to argue with Liz, of all people. But I'd only ever seen the kids working their butts off.

"So, Ms. Yuna," said Anz, "who might these people be?"

Oh! Uh, right! I introduced Liz to Anz's group and gave her the same explanation I had to the headmistress.

"They're helping at the orphanage?" asked Liz.

"Yeah, since I've been putting a burden on you and the headmistress."

"Compared to things before we met you, this is nothing. We had our hands full just trying to survive back then. We had nothing to eat and couldn't seem to *find* anything to eat. But it's different now. We have a lot on our hands, sure, but with work and will, we can always get food for the kids and ourselves. That's all thanks to you, Yuna. Even if we have our hands full, we can keep our stomachs full too."

Really? Liz was saying the same things as the headmistress. It really would be a big deal if the two of them collapsed, but they didn't seem to even be thinking about that.

From there, Liz explained what kind of work the kids were doing. Anz nodded along. "Did you make this place too, Yuna?"

"She did. When she saw the kids had empty bellies, Ms. Yuna gave them work so they could eat until they were stuffed. Thanks to her, the kids can now eat their fill."

I shrugged. "It's tit for tat. They're the reason I can get eggs."

Liz laughed. "I guess so, eh?" Had she not realized?

"Still," said Anz, "that's a lot of birds that they're taking care of."

"And you'll be able to use eggs and birds as ingredients, so make sure to cook something tasty."

"I-I'll do what I can."

I'd have Anz work her hardest to make tons of delicious meals.

140

The Bear Leads Anz and the Others to the Orphanage Part Two

ONCE WE GOT into the next shed over, where we managed the eggs, we found Fina sitting on a chair, her hands busy with something. Shuri was cleaning the egg cases next to her.

"Looks like you two really are getting things done," said Tiermina.

"Mom?" Fina whirled around. "And Anz?"

"Fina, Shuri, it's been a while!"

Fina and Shuri ran over to Anz. "Yeah, a long while!"

"We'll be seeing a lot more of each other now, though. I'm going to work at Yuna's shop from now on, and I'm looking forward to seeing you."

"Yeah, I'm looking forward to that!"

"Uh-huh, me too."

The two of them were delighted to see Anz again. Then, I introduced Neaf and the others, who would be working with Anz.

"So, what are you doing, Fina?"

"We're calculating how many eggs are left. Yuna, are you taking them?"

The number of eggs that we sold to the trade guild and the shop, at least, were set. Although, if Morin ever wanted additional eggs at the shop, we'd prioritize that order. "Does the shop have enough?"

"Yes, they already took what they needed and they got some stocked up, so they're fine."

Cool, the remaining eggs would end up going to me. If I put them in the bear storage, I could keep them fresh. I gratefully took the extra eggs.

Apparently, Liz was going to start prepping for lunch after this. "Would all of you like to eat as well?"

I looked to the group—everybody seemed pretty into it. "In that case," Anz proposed, "please let me help."

Liz gave me a troubled look. It looked like she was conflicted about whether to let a guest help or turn her down. Still, this was a good opportunity to let them get to know each other.

"Well, there's a lot of people," I said, "so can I count on you, Anz?"

"Of course!" said Anz brightly.

"Well then," said Liz, "I'm counting on you, Ms. Anz," Liz took Anz and headed into the orphanage.

I helped out the kids so we could finish up the work faster, and once we were done, we headed back to the orphanage.

"I'm going to take a quick look at how Anz is doing," said Seno. "If they look busy, I'll lend a hand." Seno headed to the kitchen. Forne and Bettle followed after her. Neaf tried to go, too, but a small boy was holding onto her hand.

"I think we're gonna be stuck playing with the kids, Neaf."

Neaf wasn't so sure. "We should help them cook."

"But..." one of the kids whimpered.

"I don't think he's gonna let go so easily."

Forne and Bettle were gone with Seno, so it was on us to play with the kids until the food was ready. The kids tugged at my clothes and hugged me. I was amazed that the headmistress and Liz could handle such rambunctious kids day in and day out. I'd explode after an hour or two for sure. As for Neaf—I was a little worried at first, but she was surrounded by kids and seemed to be enjoying herself.

Her face had seemed a little stiff at first, but I watched the smile go from glass to something far more certain.

All of the dishes that Anz and the others had made were delicious, and the kids loved them. After that, in order to make sure Neaf and the kids got to know each other better, I had her play with them and work at the orphanage for the rest of the day.

That'd be the best way for everyone to get along—working together. This was the most difficult part of any work I did for me personally, but thanks to the bear clothes, the kids liked me all right.

Seno and Forne headed over with the kids to take care of the birds, and Bettle and Neaf played with the little kid gang. Since Tiermina had things to do at the shop and trade guild, she left the orphanage. Fina and Shuri went with her. Meanwhile, Anz headed back to the shop to take inventory on what tools they'd need.

We stayed at the orphanage until twilight. The kids saw us off outside. It hadn't taken long for the kids to accept Seno and the others. In particular, the little kid gang had taken a liking to Neaf.

I guess people with kids were used to dealing with them? Made sense.

"Come again?" one of the kids squeaked.

"Of course we will," Neaf promised, dispensing tons of head pats. Everyone waved goodbye, and we headed out.

The newbies talked among themselves:

"The headmistress and Liz seemed like kind people, didn't they?"

"The kids were so well-behaved and adorable."

"There were some kids who seemed like they'd be stubborn. But they listened to the headmistress."

"Still, it really must be difficult with just the two of them."

Yeah, they'd be fine working at both the orphanage and the shop. Just as I was thinking that, Neaf looked over at me.

"What's up, Neaf?"

Neaf stopped and looked at me earnestly. "Yuna, I'd like to talk to you about something. Instead of working at the shop, could I focus most of my work on helping at the orphanage?"

At that, the rest of them stopped and looked at her. Neaf noticed. "It's not that I don't want to work with everyone else," she added. "It's just, I'd like to be with the kids..."

Neaf was trying her best to explain herself, and I got it. She just really wanted to take care of the kids. It seemed like everyone else had realized that, too, since they broke into smiles.

"Fine by me," said Seno, beaming. "The kids seemed like they liked Neaf too."

The others spoke up:

"Yeah. I have no problem with that."

"Yeah, I'm good with that."

"Are you really sure?" Neaf looked back at everyone.

"Neaf," said Bettle—she'd been playing with the little kid gang too, so she'd watched her friend carefully—"You smiled again. I mean, *really* smiled. I can't remember the last time I saw you like that."

"Yeah, I..." Seno nodded. "You've looked so strained till now."

"Did I?"

"We've all noticed," Bettle admitted.

Seno agreed. "There's been so much...awfulness. If being with the kids is what helps you after you've gone through so much, I'm happy to give you up to them."

"My friends..." Neaf couldn't finish her sentence.

"C'mon, Neaf. Go for it," I said.

Neaf looked at everyone.

"I'll tell Anz for you," I said.

"Yuna, everyone, thank you so much." Neaf's smile was as bright and true as the sun. From here on out, Neaf would work at the orphanage instead of the shop. "But I'll come to help out if the shop gets busy," she added, "so make sure you put that elbow grease in to make the place popular."

"Oh, if we do our jobs, this shop is gonna be such a hit that we'll need some helping paws."

Neaf laughed. "That sounds reassuring."

And with that, she ran back to the orphanage and those kids.

When we reported it all to Anz, she cheerfully agreed. Anz had been worried about Neaf too.

The next day, I led the group to the Bear's Lounge. There weren't customers in the morning, so I could introduce them without *too* much chaos, but I thought the shop's workers might be in the middle of prepping, so I wanted make sure we wouldn't be a bother.

"This is your shop then, Yuna?"

"And you sell bread here?"

There was a bear holding bread in front of the shop, hence the Sherlockian assessment.

"We will *not* be outdone by this bear," Seno proclaimed. "We need a fish bear."

I pretended not to hear and headed into the shop from the back entrance. Once I got inside, we found the kids in their bear jackets baking bread along with Morin and Karin.

"Yuna?!" When I got into the kitchen, one of the kids spotted me.

"That is the me."

"And it's the ladies from before?"

It looked like they remembered seeing us outside the store the other day. Jeez, they had better memories than *I* did.

"Yuna, are you having your breakfast like usual?" Morin asked.

"Yep. But can you throw in four other servings?" I'd told the others not to eat breakfast to make room for all that good, good Bear's Lounge bread.

"Please eat as much as you'd like."

"Thank you." I dug right in.

"Are these four your guests?"

"I think you already know, but they've come from Mileela to work at my other shop."

"Yes, that one. Goodness, you four sure came out a long way."

Closer than coming from the capital like Morin, though. "So, I'm introducing everyone and having them look around the shop too."

I introduced Anz's group to Morin, Karin, and the

kids. Once we got greetings out of the way, I showed them around the store.

"The inside of the shop is chock-full of bears too." They marveled at the bear decorations all over the place, from the tables to the walls. "But they're cute!"

Forne gave a table bear with a fish in its mouth a little poke. "I'd like them in our shop too."

Which meant they'd ask *me* to make them, right?

After we'd gone around looking through the shop's interior, I took advantage of Morin's offer and we feasted on fresh bread.

"Oh, this bread is delicious!"

"Yep, and all of our other bread too."

Anz nodded. "So the bread we had the other day was this, then. We couldn't stop talking about how tasty it was."

That made this bear feel all fuzzy inside.

141
The Bear Is Tired of Milaine Barging In

A FEW DAYS had passed since Anz and the others arrived.

Neaf was living in the orphanage and looking after the kids every day now. I was getting a lot of requests from Anz and the others about doing this or that to prep the shop, but it was all going smoothly. We'd bought the tools for the kitchen and decided the tableware and such. Whenever we made an order, Anz calculated the costs and went pale. Even ordering chairs had her wondering if we could get cheaper ones.

I wasn't worried about money, so I bought anything that Anz thought was necessary for the shop. Besides, you gotta spend money to make money.

And now it was the day that the tables, chairs, and stuff would arrive, so I headed for the shop.

"Please put the large table over here. The smaller tables can go here." When I got to the shop, Anz was giving out directions to set up the tables and chairs in nice, neat little rows.

"Very shop-lookin'," I said. "Everything's going well?"

"These are the new tables," Anz said, running her hand over one and smiling. "After this, once the seafood and rice arrive from Mileela, we'll be able to open the shop anytime."

Yeah—everything else was pretty much done, save stocking up on seafood.

As if summoned by the thought, Milaine barged in: "What are you talking about? Isn't there something we still need to decide on?" She loomed in the shop entrance. "Anz, it's been so long." And now she made her approach... "Yuna, Anz, aren't you both forgetting something important?"

What was she *doing* here? And had she been listening in on our conversation? I had no idea how to respond. Anz and the others looked just as surprised as me.

"Why are you here, Milaine?" Might as well start there.

"I heard from Tiermina that Anz had come to Crimonia, so I simply had to drop by. I really meant to come sooner, but I was so busy with all that tunnel work, you know."

Right—opening the tunnel would increase traffic back and forth, which would definitely make the trade guild busy too.

"What are we forgetting?" I asked.

"*Branding*, Yuna. What will you call the shop? What will the uniforms look like?"

Ohhh. Yeah, we'd been so focused on the interior design that we hadn't even thought up a name. But how did she know that? "I get you on the name, but what was that about uniforms?"

I was getting a bad feeling about this.

"It's your shop, Yuna, isn't it? So we simply *must* have uniforms."

Was it just my imagination? I feel like I heard her say "bear" just now instead of my own name. I had to just be hearing things...right?

"We *did* forget to name the place," said Anz with a nod. Oh no. Anz didn't know what she was getting herself into by going with the flow. Anz knew the professional and efficient guild master, but that was only part of the story.

Still, Milaine wasn't *wrong*. We really did need a name and a sign for the shop. Even if we did open, no one would know what kind of place this was without a sign.

"Since it's your shop, Anz," said Milaine, "you can choose a name."

"Me?"

Hold on, hadn't she just called it *my* shop? And I hadn't been able to name my *actual* shop, the Bear's Lounge! I mean, fine, maybe Anz could name it, but— what if it was *weird*?

"Yeah, you can decide it Anz," I said in a voice that hopefully didn't sound strained at all.

"Oh my gosh, this is so sudden..." Anz looked around helplessly.

"What did Deigha name his business?" I asked. "Since you've taken up Deigha's mantle of flavor, you could call this a second location? Maybe the Crimonia branch of his place?"

"Uhh, the inn doesn't have a name," said Anz.

"Really?"

Seno and the others nodded.

"I don't know its name."

"Me neither. We just called it Anz's Inn or Deigha's Inn," said Forne.

Hmm. Come to think of it, I remembered Atola calling it the Muscles Inn. If the place had an actual name that everyone kept forgetting, I actually felt pretty sorry for Deigha.

"In that case, what should we do about the shop's name?" asked Anz.

232

Like a prophet of doom, like a bearer of darkness, Milaine spoke: "I think," she intoned with grim finality, "you might as well go with a bear theme. Yuna's bakery is the Bear's Lounge, right? In that case, I think that a name with 'bear' in it would fit this shop too. And there's already a bear statue out front."

Ugh, I did *not* need this. *Was* there a bear statue holding a giant fish standing in front of the shop? Yes, but that was sheer coincidence. Seno had steamrolled me into making it! Anz and the others hadn't disagreed and had even said it might make it easier to tell it was a shop that offered seafood cuisine, so I couldn't say no. But a bear... couldn't they have just made a statue of a fish? Maybe a really cute fish?

"The Bear's Lounge is such a good name," said Anz, sort of like the politicians in a movie where they're all ignoring the smart scientist and making the wrong decision even though *nobody* should call the shop something bear-related because *come on*. "It's such a soothing shop with all the bear decorations outside and inside."

"But the vibes aren't really *lounge*-y," I said. "This isn't the type of place where you get a light meal and hibernate."

Forne gasped "Oh! Then perhaps we could call it a Bear Bistro? This shop is a restaurant, isn't it?"

"Needs more oomph," I said.

"Bear Seafood Restaurant?"

"We'll have things other than seafood too."

"Perhaps the Bear and Fish Shop?" Seno tried, uncreatively.

"The Bear's Hearty Meal Shop?"

"That kind of sounds good. It makes it sound like a place where even a bear could eat their fill."

They kept throwing more and more names out there, with more bears in each than you could shake a claw at. Finally, after we talked it through, we ended up settling on the first name—the Bear Bistro.

"In that case, I'll order the sign, if you're all right with that?"

"Sure, but please talk to Tiermina about it." Tiermina pretty much always got the last word. People would at least get my permission, but I approved just about everything. Tiermina did a thorough check so I didn't just rubber-stamp *all* of it.

"I know that," said Milaine. Her eyes flashed. "Well then, you've decided on a shop name, so now all you need to do is the uniforms."

Oh no... Milaine wasn't trying to force Anz and the other women to wear bear clothes like the kids, right? Nah, I couldn't imagine her going *that* far.

Anz blinked. "A uniform? I thought we would just wear aprons like normal."

Right? But I didn't say anything.

"Yes, but that's not entertain—err, wouldn't fit with the image of the Bear Bistro." (She was just gonna keep going like I never heard that with my infinitely sharp bear ears, huh?) "I think that this definitely calls for bear clothes."

All four women stood silently, finally realizing what Milaine was going for.

The rumor was that the Bear's Lounge's uniform had been *my* idea, because wasn't it supposed to be my shop? There was no escaping hearsay.

They hadn't expected this treachery from Milaine.

"You're going to have us wear bear clothes..." Anz frowned. "...like the kids?"

"I can't!" Forne blurted.

"That's a little... Considering my age..." Bettle wore a strained smile.

"I think I might want to give it a try," said Seno.

Ripples of shock ran across the room. Even Milaine looked surprised. I mean, everyone other than Seno had turned the proposal down, which made me feel weirdly bad, to be honest, like they were kinda rejecting how I dressed.

"I don't think we need anything special," said Anz. "Just our normal clothes and an apron."

"That won't do!" Milaine cried, practically hopping up and down. "Branding! It's Yuna's shop, and we need *branding*!"

Anz gave her a bewildered look. She *was* the trade guild's master, so they couldn't challenge her. Milaine had rehabilitated Mileela's trade guild as well, and she had done *so* much for Mileela. She'd even arranged for their food. Crimonia's trade guild had been at the heart of the development around the tunnel too. Could they really turn down someone to whom they owed so much when she was right in front of them?

I think even I would struggle. Milaine was practically unstoppable when she put her mind to something. That was why the Bear's Lounge had ended up with that bear uniform.

Anz looked at me, hoping for help. "Milaine, none of them seem like they're on board."

"Aww. But Anz...I got this prepped specially for youuuuu..." Milaine pulled a big ol' adult-sized bear jacket from her item bag. Had she really gone out of her way to make it? "Won't you please try it on? Pleaaaaaase?"

"No, um. I'm sorry," said Anz with hardly a glance.

Wh-what was that? I felt a pang in my heart. She couldn't bear to be a bear... Ouch.

Milaine seemed disappointed, but she didn't give up. In the end, we went with aprons embroidered with bears—a nice(?) compromise.

Anz looked dead tired by the end of it. Internally, I was putting my hands together and offering her my prayers in condolence, but I was pretty much knocked out myself. Every time someone rejected a bear, I took just a teensy bit of psychic damage.

KUMA
KUMA
KUMA
BEAR

142
The Bear Orders Embroidery

WE WERE DECIDED: Anz and the others would work in aprons embroidered with bears. But that got me thinking. There was the orphan girl a while back who'd embroidered a cushion for me. That big, bear-embroidered cushion had come in handy when I'd been a guard for the academy. Thanks to that thing, I'd been able to travel in that carriage in comfort.

"Milaine," I said, "about the embroidery. Where are you going to get it done?"

"I'm planning to ask the tailors who did the Bear's Lounge uniforms. What about that?"

"I've got this thing that one of the girls at the orphanage made for me." I pulled out the cushion with bear embroidery from my bear storage and showed Milaine the little cartoon bear.

"Wh-what is that?!" Milaine stuck out her hand and snatched the cushion from me.

"A girl named Sherry from the orphanage gave it to me."

"Why, it's simply adorable. And such fine work." Milaine touched the embroidery hungrily. Even in my eyes, the bear was cartoony enough to look cute. I suspected Sherry had used the ornaments in the shop as references.

"Right? So if you're going to ask for things to be embroidered, why don't you ask this girl to do it?" Sherry was nimble with her hands and was always sewing in the corner of a room. The cushions and curtains of the orphanage were decorated with embroidery, all Sherry's handiwork. She'd given me a towel, too, and it was just as cute.

Forne stared at the cushion. "Are we really going to wear these bear aprons while working?"

"How cute."

"But isn't it embarrassing?"

"Yeah, a little."

The only person who seemed totally on board was Seno. The other three seemed too embarrassed to go along with it.

Milaine gave the three a scheming look. "In that case, would you prefer the same clothes as the children?"

Aaaaand just like that, they were all enthusiasm.

"N-no, an apron with this embroidery is fine."

"I'm fine with it too."

"Right. It's nice and cute."

"Yeah, I'm fine with an apron too...I think."

Milaine clapped her hands and giggled. "In that case, let's have Sherry do the embroidery."

Agree and get an apron or disagree for a bear outfit... brutal.

With that decided, Milaine and I immediately headed to the orphanage to see Sherry.

Sherry's job was taking care of the birds, so we headed to the henhouse. It looked like everyone was taking a break and playing for the moment. I asked one of the kids about Sherry and found that she'd headed back to the orphanage.

Inside, I found Neaf talking with the headmistress and Liz.

"Sherry? She should be in her room on the second floor."

We made our way there, knocked—

"Sherry, are you in?"

And headed in.

"Yuna?" A girl of about twelve sat on a bed, embroidering—this was Sherry, of cushion-and-curtains fame.

"Could I talk to you for a minute?"

"Yeah, sure." Sherry was a little nervous at this sudden surprise. It was probably Milaine putting her on edge. The guild master had a habit of mildly terrorizing people, after all.

"Were you embroidering?" I asked.

"Yeah. I like doing it." In fact, she was holding a half-finished piece right there in her hands.

"Could you show me?" Milaine and I peeked at Sherry's hands. She was embroidering a cartoon bear like the ones at the Bear's Lounge.

"A bear, huh?"

"Mmhm! I was hoping it could be a decoration for the shop."

"I think you could even sell this," Milaine said with a gleam in her eye.

"You're pretty good."

"Pretty...good..." Sherry blushed, but she seemed happy.

Milaine took charge. "We have something to ask you. Are you ready?" She held onto Sherry's small hands as she explained about the shop aprons.

"You want me to do that..." Sherry looked flabbergasted.

I nodded. "Yeah, think we can count on you?"

"But..."

Sherry turned her face down. I came closer to her and Milaine stepped back. If she didn't want to do it, I didn't want to force her, but... "Hey. If you don't want to do it, that's okay, all right? Do you not want to?"

"Nuh-uh, that's not it. But..."

"But?" Then what was wrong?

"What if people don't like my embroidery and it makes them stop going to the shop? And then we won't be able to buy food, and...and the orphanage will go away, and..." Sherry looked dead serious. That was what she was thinking? I know I wasn't supposed to, but I couldn't help but smile. She cared so much about her home, about Liz and the headmistress, about Neaf, about everyone...

"Sherry, it's all right." I gently patted Sherry's head with my bear puppet.

"Yuna?"

"The shop wouldn't go belly up because of something like that. I'm setting it up, after all. You remember how the bakery was flooded with customers, right?"

"Yeah."

"And the eggs are selling, right?"

"Yeah."

"Well, it's the same me making this shop. And it's the same me that wants your embroidery. This bear isn't gonna let something bad like that happen, you hear?"

"But I..." she started.

I pulled the cushion Sherry had given me from my bear storage.

She gasped. "That's..."

"It is. I was so happy when you gave this to me. I think it's really well made. Won't you make some aprons with cute bears like this? I know you can do it."

"Yuna..." Sherry raised her face slightly.

One more push would do the trick. "Anyway, if anything goes wrong, it'll be Milaine's fault. Since it was Milaine's idea. But if things go well, then it's all thanks to you."

"Wai—" Milaine coughed. "Um. Yuna?"

Whatever *that* was could wait. "And hey, this cushion?" I gave the little embroidered bear a poke. "Too cute to fail."

"Are you sure you're fine with me doing it though? I'm just an amateur."

"Amateur shmamateur," I said. "You'd be surprised at how fast you can pick stuff up."

Sherry bit her bottom lip. She thought it over, struggled, then came up with her answer. "Yeah, okay. I'll do it. I'll work really hard for you, Yuna." She finally raised her face.

"Thank you." I gave her another pat on the head.

Sherry broke into a full smile, but there was somebody around to spoil the mood.

"In that case, I'll be taking you with me, Sherry," Milaine said, totally killing the vibe as she wrapped her arm around the kid's waist.

"Um, Yuna?" Sherry strained against Milaine, looking puzzled.

"Milaine?!"

"We have business at the tailor, she and I. I'm going to talk to them about the aprons, so I need her, don't I? So I'll be taking Sherry." She tugged on Sherry's hand again.

"Eep! We're going *where*?"

Unable to resist Milaine's sinister might, Sherry was yoinked out of the room, asking confused questions all the way.

I made sure to tell Liz that Milaine had taken Sherry and that she'd need to bow out of taking care of the birds for a while.

KUMA
KUMA
KUMA
BEAR

143
The Bear Opens Shop

A FEW DAYS HAD PASSED since Milaine had taken Sherry and, finally, the embroidered aprons came in. I was impressed she'd been able to make them in such a short time. She hadn't just made four for the women working at the shop, either—she'd even prepped one for Neaf, since she'd be coming by to help out now and again. The couple who managed the tailor shop had apparently been shocked by Sherry's speed.

Sherry hadn't only helped with the embroidery but with making the aprons themselves. She'd been good at sewing from the start—for a while now, Sherry had been mending the orphan's torn clothes in the headmistress's place. They probably hadn't even been able to buy clothes before I came into the picture, so mending had been a given.

Sherry continued going to the tailor even after she finished the aprons. The shop couple had apparently invited her to work at their shop from then on. Even though Sherry hesitated at first, the headmistress encouraged her not to miss a good opportunity, so she decided to take the job.

I guess she still wasn't all that confident, since she was still muttering, "Are you sure you want me...?"

Still, she seemed happy that others had recognized the skills her mom had taught her when she was young. I didn't know how far she'd get, but I heard she was going to learn how to make clothes and tons of other things too.

Sherry told me all of this bashfully.

"Looks like someone finally noticed what you can do and how hard you work," I said, and she beamed.

Prep for the shop was well underway and Anz's group was working hard to get it open.

I was putting some elbow grease into it, too, of course. I made bears for outside the shop, I made bears for inside the shop, I made bears for outside the shop, and I made bears for inside the shop. (They were very important, everybody said, so I just *had* to tell you a few extra times.)

In addition to the bear at the entrance to the shop—the one with the giant fish to show this was a shop that made fish-based cuisine—I also made bears to put inside the shop. I was gonna have to make bears anyway, so I figured I might as well make a few extra—no escape, you know? So I made a statue of a bear hunkering down in a sitting position with a bowl and chopsticks.

Seemed a little cluttered, but what did I know? I just made 'em.

Finally, it was the day before the Bear Bistro's opening. We'd sourced the main seafood and rice ingredients from Mileela. The ice mana gems I'd taken off the snow-min from the Elezent mountain range were coming in handy—normal adventurers would have had trouble getting those things, but not me.

Those same mountains were why Mileela and Crimonia used to have so much trouble intermingling. But now the tunnel was done, and people could trade or commute—all of which was making a positive influence on both places, according to Cliff.

The trade guild and adventurers' guild had joined together to make it all happen too, though Cliff was the one giving out most of the directions. Felt a little weird to think about that, even if the trade guild was also involved; the guild was selling the seafood and salt, but salt production and sales happened at Cliff's command and under the king's jurisdiction.

I didn't know the details of how they made salt from saltwater, but (according to novels and manga I'd read) it was supposed to be some harsh manual labor.

So, when I heard about the salt, I'd told them not to cause trouble for the residents in Mileela. Just in case, I'd let it slip to Cliff that, "If anything happens, the tunnel might end up naturally collapsing on itself."

I'm very subtle when I need to be.

But Cliff probably wouldn't do anything fishy, so I wasn't all *that* worried.

We'd also revved up publicity for the grand opening of the shop. I'd asked Milaine to put up flyers at the trade guild and other relevant venues. Tiermina had told me she asked the butcher and the grocer we worked with to put some up as well.

I did a sample tasting at the Bear's Lounge too. Anz prepped the fish, and made seafood dishes, hand rolls, bamboo shoot rice, and seasoned rice for people to try for free. Lastly, we made seafood hotpot and distributed it to the customers.

Like I said, you've got to spend some to make some. No matter how great your food is, it's hard to get people to spend money on something new. On the other hand, if they try it for free and like it, they'll come by and pay next time. If those initial customers told other people about it after, we were looking at a huge success. There was no way anyone could fail to recognize how great Anz's food was, even after a single taste.

Just like I thought, we had a ton of customers on opening day. I had Rulina and Gil guard the front of the shop just like I had with the Bear's Lounge. The agreement was that they'd get a week of meals in return. Since I had two adventurers standing at the entrance, nobody made a scene, and we didn't see any kind of ruckus.

I helped out in the back too. They taught me how to prep the fish, but I wasn't as good as Anz and the others. I helped more with the veggie and meat dishes.

The seasoned rice-style dishes were unexpectedly popular. I guess folks liked the soy sauce, since those items were practically flying out of our kitchen. The soy sauce also attracted people to the seafood, which got us some promising orders.

Once the day ended, all the people in the shop seemed dead. Neaf had come to help from the orphanage, but it had been so busy that now, at the end of the day, she was collapsed over a table. Anz, Bettle, and I had made the food while Forne and Seno had worked hard at the front of the shop.

"I'm beat."

"I'm going to die."

"I had no idea it'd be so busy."

"I'd like to ask for a raise."

Everyone looked resentfully at me. Way to put me on the spot. I was pretty sure I'd warned them from the start how popular this would get, given how good Anz was at cooking, but the first taste menu had earned a bigger response than even I expected.

"If you're going to blame anyone, blame Anz," I groaned. "This all happened because she went all-out for the food tasting."

"But Yuna, I wanted to have lots of people try the food."

"Then you think you can keep this shop running, Anz?"

Anz nodded. "I was anxious at first, but I'm happy that so many people are excited to try my food."

"But it was so hectic," Neaf mumbled. "Too many..."

I shook my head. "For now, sure. People will come from far away because the food is novel, but once fish and rice start going around, they'll be able to eat it at all kinds of other establishments. Things'll settle down then, and it'll be a battle between you and a bunch of upstarts. That's when you'll really have to show off your skills, Anz."

"I'll put my heart into it," Anz said, managing more gusto than I thought could fit into someone so exhausted.

Yeah. She was gonna be okay.

KUMA
KUMA
KUMA
BEAR

144
The Bear Tries to Get the Black Tiger Harvested

Anz's shop was getting good foot traffic. It wasn't as hectic as the first day, though. Rice and fish had started selling in a bunch of places, and other Mileelans like Anz had come to open their own shops in Crimonia. Inevitable, I guess.

I was happy for seafood to spread throughout Crimonia. As long as Anz worked hard to keep the shop from flopping, things would be all right—and no way would she lose out to those upstarts. Not Anz, the great successor to Deigha.

Sure, something *could* come up, but—nah, Anz wasn't the type to get conceited and get lazy. Even if not being arrogant *enough* threatened her, Seno and the others would back her up. If push came to shove, we could rely on all my secret hot tips from my home world—umm, ideally. Even if it was mostly surface-level knowledge...

Why hadn't I studied cooking back home?!

The shop had also settled down, so I was hoping to finally get that dead black tiger (remember him?) harvested. I had been so busy after my guarding mission— with Anz coming to Crimonia and the shop prep—that I hadn't had time to dress the black tiger and get its pelt.

Fina was coming to my bear house in order to take care of it today. It was always a little weird to me, asking a ten-year-old girl to harvest monsters, but she'd done it hundreds of times, so it was too late to worry *too* much about that.

Plus, it wasn't like Fina *had* to take the work these days. Tiermina was healthy, working, and had remarried, so Fina had her new dad, Gentz. Fina didn't *need* to work, but she didn't turn me down and I couldn't quite get myself to give up her skills. So...as long as Fina didn't say anything or seem like she didn't want to do it, I wasn't going to revoke our agreement.

Soon enough, Fina showed up. "Yuna, good morning!"

She always had so much energy. Made me smile. "Mornin', Fina."

"So, what did you need me to do?"

When I'd first asked Fina to do the harvesting for me, there had been people around, so I hadn't been able to tell her it was a black tiger. All I'd said was that I needed something from her and that she should come by the bear house.

"There's a monster I want you to harvest."

"Is it a wolf harvest?"

"Close, I guess?" Black tigers were more similar to wolves than you'd think, though their size and color were a little different.

Uh. In my opinion, anyway.

I took Fina over to the bear-shaped storehouse next to my bear-shaped house. There, I pulled the black tiger out of my bear storage. It made a sort of hefty thunking sound when I set it on the table. Its weight distribution was definitely different than a wolf's, in any case.

"Y-Yuna?!" Fina yelped.

Well, of course she'd be surprised. She looked at the black tiger, then at me.

I shrugged. "I killed a black tiger. Think you could harvest it? I'll pay you, obviously, soooooo..."

Fina stared at the black tiger.

"What's up, Fina? You can do it, right?"

"Um. Dad said that wolves, tigerwolves, and black tigers are closely related monsters, so you harvest them the same way. I think that I know how to harvest it. But there might be another reason why it's out of my league." Fina touched the black tiger.

Since tigerwolves were supposed to be greater monsters, I'd thought she'd be able to take care of this one. I guess I'd need to take it to the adventurers' guild then.

Fina took her hands off the body. "Can I take a stab at it?"

"Go for it."

Fina pulled out her harvesting knife from her item bag and took a literal stab at the black tiger's stomach. But when she tried to move her knife, it wouldn't budge.

"Ughhh," Fina groaned. No matter how firmly she attempted to cut, the knife wouldn't move at all. Fina gave up and let go. "Yuna, I think I really can't do it."

"Is it too tough to harvest?" Actually yeah, when we'd fought, its skin *had* been pretty tough...

"Yeah, my knife isn't strong enough to actually do any cutting..."

So the issue wasn't Fina's harvesting skills and stuff—it was that she needed a better tool. "What if you had a sharper knife?"

"Oh, um, I could probably do it the same as the tigerwolves, then."

Simple enough, then: If it was the knife that couldn't

do its part, then I just needed to prep her a knife that could. "In that case, how about we go buy a knife that can harvest a black tiger?"

"Yuna, that kind of knife is super expensive. You can't *buy* one." Fina cocked her head to the side and tried to appeal to me, but it was no use.

"Don't worry about it. It'll be thanks for doing all that harvesting for me. C'mon, let's go."

I stowed the black tiger back in my bear storage, grabbed Fina's hand with my bear puppet's mouth, and the two of us headed to the blacksmith where I'd first bought my knives and sword months ago. When we got inside, a somewhat short woman welcomed us—Nelt was her name. The smithy was run by a dwarf couple.

"Welcome. Oh, goodness—if it isn't Fina and the bear lass. What brings you here today?"

"We came here to buy a new harvesting knife for Fina."

"For Fina? I thought that we sharpened Fina's knife just the other day. Did it break?" Nelt asked.

"No, um, it didn't break."

"Then why would Fina need a new harvesting knife?"

"We had a monster that an iron knife can't handle, so we want something sharper than iron."

"Gracious, what in the world are you trying to harvest? A dragon?"

Was it okay to tell her? She wasn't going to make a big deal out of it, was she?

"I won't know until you tell me," she added. "You defeated a black viper. It's too late to hold back now."

"Just please keep it a secret." She agreed, and I explained about the black tiger.

She chuckled. "There you go, fighting ridiculous monsters again. But a black tiger, you say? An iron knife really wouldn't work for that. You either need one made of steel or mithril."

Oooh, mithril! Now that's *what I call fantasy stuff.* The game had had all kinds of mithril gear. Ahh, how nostalgic. Still, I'd had no idea that mithril existed here too.

Yep, I had to go with... "I'll take one mithril knife, please." And maybe a sword, if they had one. Even if it was a little pricey, it was a *mithril sword.* I mean, come on.

Fina grabbed my arm and shook me. "Yuna, mithril knives are expensive. Way more than steel, and steel's super expensive too!"

"Nope, I'm going with mithril," I said firmly. "We'll probably need it sooner or later."

Fina's jaw dropped. "What in the world are you planning to have me harvest...?"

Nelt had mentioned dragons earlier, right? That'd be

cool. Or maybe some big monster with a shell? Who could say?

"Sorry," said Nelt. "I wish I could sell you one, but alas. We're currently out of our mithril supply."

"You don't have any?"

Seemed it really *was* rare. I still wanted it, expensive or not...

"A steel knife would be able to cut through the monster though."

"No, I'd like a mithril knife," I said plainly.

"Yes, dear, but I think it will be difficult for you to get one in this town."

"It will?"

"Mithril's a rare ore, and we currently have a shortage of *all* our ores. That's why we're not sure when we'll get mithril."

"So it's not just mithril, then?"

"We have some other ores stockpiled for now, so it hasn't started much of a commotion yet. We're running low or out of all the scarcer varieties, though."

Come to think of it, I remembered that when we'd tried to buy more kitchen utensils for Anz's shop, Tiermina had said the price had gone up. I'd just ignored it at the time, but was this the reason it had been more expensive? "But why is there a shortage?"

I'd heard that places would gather all their iron in case of war, but this country didn't have any wars going on, right?

"It seems that there was an issue at the mines, and they can't excavate more."

"What's the issue?"

"I didn't hear that part. I think the trade guild would know more details."

Hm. It wasn't like I'd get a mithril knife just by figuring out the reason behind the shortage. Maybe a capital blacksmith would have them? I had the bear transport gate, so maybe I'd pop by. "Thanks. I'll pop over to the capital then."

"All the way to the capital?! Oh, I suppose you have those bear summons. In that case, please give me a moment."

Nelt was taken aback for a sec, but she was close enough in the end. I couldn't tell her about the transport gate, so I just nodded. She headed into a back room, and there was a noise like she was giving Gold a light thump to wake him up.

A short commotion, some brief quiet, and right when I was wondering if something was up, Nelt came back like nothing was the matter. "Thank you for your patience. Take this with you." She handed me a letter.

"And this is?"

"If you're headed to the capital, there's a smithy managed by a man named Ghazal. Try heading there, though I think he'll be more accommodating if you give this to him."

"Ghazal, you say?"

"He's from the same area as me." A dwarf, then, right? "But they may be running low on ore, too, so don't get your hopes up."

"That's fine—thank you so much." After expressing my gratitude, I took the letter and the two of us left the store. I put my hand on Fina's head. "Wanna head to the capital?"

"Right now?!"

"I have the bear transport gate. Why not?"

"I guess you're right..."

"Is there an issue or something?"

"Nah. Just that normally people can't go to the capital whenever they want."

"Then what's the problem? We could even tour the capital again if you want." I grabbed Fina's hand and headed back to the bear house, and from there we made straight for the transport gate.

145

The Bear Heads to the Capital in Search of a Mithril Knife

With that, we journeyed to the capital in search of a mithril knife. (The journey was, admittedly, like two minutes. Gotta love bear transport gates.) Fina and I left the bear house, and boom.

"Whoa, the capital." Fina sounded pretty chipper now. I'd been to the city loads of times, but Fina hadn't seen it since the birthday celebration. "It kind of feels strange. I can't believe we were just in Crimonia."

"It's been a while since you've been. Wanna stop by somewhere?" It wasn't like I was in a hurry.

"Nah. I'd have fun just poking around a little. It's okay." She was right. Just wandering on foot was another way of enjoying things. If we headed to a tourist spot, we could hang back and enjoy the scenery.

I'd wanted to do just that on the way to the smithy Nelt had mentioned, but, well, I actually had no idea where the guy was. I'd asked Nelt, but she'd told me she didn't know, and that was that. She just said he'd be registered at the trade guild, so I could ask them. So, that's where we went.

We were on the capital's main street, a broad thoroughfare with carriage traffic that went back and forth. To get to the trade guild, we had to follow that big ol' road down to it. There was a ton of foot traffic, which meant a whole lot people staring at me and saying familiar stuff.

Some mom never taught her kid not to point.

Somebody over there looked downright thunderstruck.

And come on, really? That one over there was gonna *laugh*?

And no, they didn't sell this at a clothing shop, yeesh.

You there, why d'you even want to order your own set?

Yup, I'm a bear. Yup, it's embarrassing. But I've given up.

You think I'm cute? Thank you.

You want a hug? *No*, thank you.

You're going to tell your friends? Please don't.

Did you just say you'll keep an eye on me so they can run? I'm not about to rip 'em to shreds or anything.

Or what, you trying to poach me for a zoo? Nope, keep your grimy hands away or I'll rip 'em off.

It was fun to answer all that stuff in my head.

Before long, we caught sight of the large building that housed the trade guild—just sizeable enough for the great capital city. Big as it was, there were still way more people than you'd think, which meant more stares.

Well, Yuna, no turning back now... I took Fina into the trade guild and the moment I did—

"Ms. Yuna!"

I heard a voice from behind me. When I turned, wondering who it was, I found Shia, Maricks, Timol, and Cattleya, all out of breath. What were these students doing here?

"Shia? Guys? What's going on?"

Shia's hair was a mess, I guess because she'd run here. "That's what I'm wondering. Why are you in the capital with Fina?"

Yeah, I supposed it was normal for the four of *them* to be in the capital, considering they lived here. I was the one out of place.

Fina bowed her head and greeted Shia, seeming a little nervous. They'd gotten to know each other a bit earlier, but Shia was still an aristocrat and Fina was a commoner, and a little hanging out couldn't change that.

After she said her hello, Fina hid behind me. She seemed a little put on the spot. But then, she didn't know anyone other than Shia. Speaking of which..."So, how are you all?"

"Pretty good."

"It's been such a long time, Yuna."

"Yuna, long time no see."

They all returned enthusiastic greetings. But there was something that bugged me. I looked at Maricks. "What's with that bruise on your face, Maricks?"

"Oh, this thing?" Maricks touched his purple left cheek. "My dad socked me one. He said I put everyone in danger by being self-centered and I disrespected your directions. He was all 'who do you think you are?'"

"He hit you because of that?"

Maricks smiled while he rubbed his cheek. "I mean, he wasn't totally wrong, you know? But he also told me he was proud of me. He said it was better to do *something* than to look the other way when someone was in trouble. But he said I gotta act only after taking my own abilities and my companion's abilities into account. Think of who I'd be up against and stuff."

Come to think of it, Ellelaura had said the same thing. But Maricks couldn't have done anything about it. No one could've expected a black tiger to appear. Maricks had acted thinking he was facing mere goblins, which he could beat. I didn't think anyone would have been so reckless if they'd known a black tiger was waiting for them.

"Still," said Shia, "I was so surprised when I saw you, Maricks. Your face was swollen when you came to the academy the next day."

Cattleya nodded. "It was much worse earlier."

"I was wondering what had happened," added Timol.

"It's better now?" I asked. I guess it really had been a bit since I'd been on guard duty. But the bruise was there even now, which meant...just how hard had Maricks's dad hit him? It looked like it'd still hurt to touch. "You okay?"

"Yeah, I'm fine. It just aches a little." Maricks smoothed his cheek lightly.

Shia rolled her eyes. "Sure, Maricks. You made such a huge deal when someone brushed it just the tiniest bit."

Cattleya nodded. "He was crying and everything."

"Of course he was," I said. "Obviously it'd hurt if someone touched it the day after he got hit." I mean, it was a swollen face. Just imagining it made my own cheek hurt. Weird how just seeing a bruise did that. "Were the rest of you fine? Did you get in trouble?"

"We did get into a little trouble with our teacher and Lady Ellelaura."

"My mother scolded me for not supporting you."

"I got in trouble for no good reason. They said it was my duty to stop Maricks. It's not like I'm Maricks's guardian or anything," Timol sulked.

"But you guys didn't get hit. That's so unfair," Maricks grumbled. "You could punch yourselves?" he said suddenly, offering a lopsided grin, and we broke into laughter.

Hmm. Maricks *had* been serving as the party leader, so he was responsible for everyone's actions. I guess that's why his dad had done it? Pretty different from Japanese parents, who were thinking less about, uh, fighting monsters and more about education.

And besides, if the parents had said, "My son wasn't in the wrong. It was the adventurer who guarded him that was at fault," or something like that, I definitely would've had to cash in that favor with Ellelaura or the king.

"So why are you in the capital with Fina?" asked Maricks.

"We're shopping. I just kind of wanted a harvesting knife."

"You came all the way to the capital to buy a harvesting knife?"

The four of them looked exasperated. I guess anybody would if they didn't know about the bear transport gate.

"Uh, I also had free time?"

"Do normal people come all the way to the capital just because they're free?"

"Well, I've got Kumayuru and Kumakyu, so I can get here really easily." When all else failed, it was time for loads more lies.

"I think it's fine because it's you, Yuna," said Timol, "but it's dangerous for two girls to be going on a journey alone." Timol and Cattleya were looking at us in shock, and, sure, maybe it would be for a normal couple of girls from Crimonia, but this was us.

"Yuna's got the bears," Maricks said, coming in for the save.

"I suppose you are right," said Cattleya with a wistful sigh. "Yuna does indeed have fuzzy, wuzzy little Kumayuru and Kumakyu... Oh, how I miss them!"

I mean? It hadn't really been that long?

"There was the black tiger I defeated when I guarded you all, right? Well, we can't harvest it with an iron knife. I was thinking of buying something better in Crimonia, but I couldn't find anything. I heard that there's a dwarven blacksmith named Ghazal, so I came here to buy one from him."

When I said that, Shia put her hand on her forehead and started to think. Then she hit her fist against her palm. "Yes! Yes, I know him."

"You do, Shia?"

"Yes, I've gone to him once before. I can take you, if you'd like?"

271

Maricks nodded. "Yeah, I know him too. It's that dwarf, huh? I think my dad was saying he was a really skilled blacksmith or something."

"I'd be glad if you did, guys, but weren't you all in the middle of something?"

"Nah, it'll be quick," said Maricks. "You're all fine with that, too, right?"

"Of course."

"Fine by me too."

"After how much you took care of us, it's the least we could do," the gang of students told me.

Hey, I wasn't gonna argue.

I turned to look at the trade guild, where we'd planned to go. I mean, I sure loved having an excuse not to go into that crowd...and all those *stares*. Ugh, no thanks.

146
The Bear Heads to the Blacksmith

SHIA AND THE OTHERS took me along to the dwarven blacksmith Ghazal. "You guys were on the way back from the academy? It kind of seems early for that though."

They were wearing their school uniforms. I had no idea when school ended, but it wasn't even lunchtime yet.

"We got classes off today, so we were planning to go monster-slaying in the woods nearby."

"Yeah, we registered at the adventurers' guild."

"We're doing it to gain experience. We don't want a repeat of what happened last time or anything."

"Last time?" I laughed. "I don't think you're in a place to beat a black tiger even if you work hard—not any time soon, anyway."

"Yeah, no," said Maricks firmly. "We're not going after some kinda horror like that. Maybe we could get strong enough to hold our own against one. We at least want to get stronger so we can protect ourselves."

"Hence the adventurers' guild-ing?"

"Yeah, but it was hard convincing my dad to let me." Apparently, he almost earned another smack, had to fight his dad off with a sword, and even had to learn more tactics before the old man would okay it. It seemed like there had been all kinds of trouble involved.

Timol shook his head. "I'm the one who had it hard. Maricks's dad is one of the knight commanders, but my dad works at the ministry of finance. Even though I was invited by Maricks, my dad really didn't want to let me even temporarily join up."

Maricks rolled his eyes. "I already apologized a ton for that."

"Looks like all of you have had it tough," said Cattleya.

"What about you, Shia?" I asked.

"I got permission from my mother by keeping it a secret from my father," she said. Oof. Cliff's own daughter hadn't even talked to him about it. "But the conditions are that we can only take quests for lesser monsters in the woods nearby."

According to them, said woods only had weak monsters

and beasts like wolves. They called them the "beginner woods" and only adventurers of F- and E-Rank were allowed in it, all to help the capital's adventurers develop their skills.

If the lower-ranked monsters around the capital dried up, local beginner adventurers would have no way to improve, and they'd have trouble cultivating homegrown talent. The adventurers' guild was really putting thought into their management of the area.

Actually, I remembered getting in trouble for over-hunting the wolves in Crimonia. Helen had asked me to mind a quota on the number of wolves I hunted for the sake of the novice adventurers, even though I had also been a novice back then. Same thing, it seemed.

"So you all got to Rank E?"

"Oh, yeah, at the least."

"Wow." Well, they'd killed goblins without a sweat, so they were capable enough.

"You're in Rank C even though you're younger, aren't you?" asked Maricks. "Getting praise from you isn't exactly..."

Excuse me, what was that? *Younger*? Looked like Maricks was lacking in eyesight just as much as he was in gray matter. Did this world have ophthalmologists? 'Cause he sure needed one before his eyes went.

I'd shown him my guild card before, hadn't I? Hadn't he looked at my age?

"I suppose you're right," said Timol. "It's not that great getting praise from Yuna when she's a kid *and* in Rank C."

Wow, an epidemic of bad eyesight. Very grim.

"I agree," said Cattleya, "but we just became adventurers. There's not much we can do about it."

The jabs kept coming and they wouldn't stop. Shia, the only one who knew my actual age, just smiled.

This was a matter of my honor. I had to correct them. "Listen up for a sec, would you?"

"What is it?"

"How old do you all think I am?"

"You're thirteen, aren't you?"

"Maybe fourteen, right?"

"Considering guild regulations, you must be thirteen. Since you can't be younger than that."

Shia choked down peals of laughter.

"Uhh, looking at me, what makes you think I'm thirteen?" (I thrust out my chest—you know, like how frogs try to look big.)

Maricks blinked. "You can't be even *younger*, can you?!"

Timol shook his head. "There's no way, Maricks. The regulations."

"Yuna," said Cattleya, shocked, "surely you didn't fake your age..."

The three looked at me dubiously.

"I'm fifteen. Fif! Teen! Fifteen! One and a half decades!"

They all froze.

"Fifteen?" I repeated, like a mantra. "My age? The number?"

Maricks tilted his head. "Uhh, Yuna, are you the same age as us?"

"I am."

"Surely you jest," said Cattleya.

Timol nodded wisely. "Of course. I should've known: Yuna...why didn't you tell us you're an elf?"

"Elf? I'm not—I'm not like, a Legolas. Just a *regular* lass. Look." I pointed at my ears. "No pointy." Even if I *was* a human from another world—I mean, come on.

"Shia, did you know?!"

"Yeah. I asked her when we first met."

"And!" I managed to calm myself like the wise elf they apparently thought I was. "Ahem. I showed you all my guild card earlier."

"I was hung up on your class back then."

"I was focused on your guild rank."

"Ah, I'm pretty sure I couldn't see it because of your bear hands." Timol looked at my bear puppets.

Ohh. I'd been holding it when I showed it to them. In that case, they might not have been able to see the top where my name was printed...and my age.

"But really, you're the same age as me? I can hardly believe it."

"Yeah." Timol squinted at my ears for a moment.

Ugh, I'm just a little small for my age. It's not rocket science, jeez...

We left the wide thoroughfare and headed down a road with some real industrial-looking buildings. Made sense. A blacksmith wouldn't be pounding iron all day in the middle of the residential area, not without noise complaints.

"Harvesting a black tiger, though..." said Maricks. "You can't do it with a normal knife?"

"Naw, I totally can. I came allllll the way to the capital city to buy a mithril knife as a joke—no, Maricks, I can't."

Cattleya nodded. "That makes sense. If typical blades could pierce a black tiger's hide, it wouldn't be so difficult to defeat them."

"Yeah, Maricks," said Shia, "open a book for once in your life."

"Okay, okay! I was just asking," he said, grumping Maricksly as the others poked at him. "But mithril, huh? That's cool. I'd like a mithril sword sometime."

"You're getting ahead of yourself, Maricks," said Timol.

Cattleya nodded. "Far too early for you."

"I agree," said Shia.

"What is with you all? My dad said the same thing, but you know? If I had a cool mithril sword in my hand—wha-chow!" Maricks swung an imaginary sword. "I'd be a little better, eh?"

Timol rolled his eyes. "I don't think it's the sword that's your problem, Maricks."

At last we arrived at the blacksmith, set up in a section of the industrial district. "Thanks, guys—you can drop me off here if you want. You need to go to the woods, don't you?"

The student gang looked at each other, as if trying to make up their minds.

"You're right," said Maricks finally. "We can't always get together, so we've got to use our time while we can."

Cattleya sighed. "Very well. Though I was actually hoping to have Yuna bring out her bears."

Aha! So Cattleya had wanted to see Kumayuru and Kumakyu. And Shia was nodding along too. I'd uncovered their secret cuddling plot.

Eh, fair enough. As thanks for them taking me all the way to the blacksmith, I summoned my bears in cub form and let the two pet them. After getting in their fair share of good, fuzzy cuddles, the two looked satisfied enough to head off to the beginner woods.

As for Timol and Maricks, they were definitely, absolutely not jealous. You could tell that they weren't jealous because of how incredibly serious and manly and *extremely* not jealous they looked.

"Well then, how about we head inside?"

"Yes," said Fina, letting out a nervous breath.

Fina and I walked in the door. It was pretty dark, but I could see swords and armor glimmering on the walls. This guy didn't just focus on weapons.

"Um, is anyone here?" Spooky. I didn't see anyone, so I called out. A short man wobbled out from the back. Based on that height, he was definitely a dwarf.

"Are you Ghazal?"

"Ghazal, yes, I am. And who are you? Why are you in those queer clothes?"

Wow, okay, cool. Pretty tactless, my guy. "Leave my clothes out of it, please. Could you take a look at this?"

I handed over the letter I'd received from Nelt.

Ghazal stared at my bear puppet hand...or...the letter? I couldn't tell.

"It's a letter from Nelt and Gold from Crimonia," he muttered. That's what I'd thought. Why else would Nelt go to the back and whack Gold awake? Ghazal took the letter from the bear puppet and solemnly read. "Young woman, I understand why you're here, but I'm afraid that you ask the impossible. We have a mithril shortage in the capital as well."

"Even here?"

"The closest mineral vein...we can no longer rely on it. I could make your knife with iron or even another material, but not mithril. It's scarce, and I've no way to obtain more. In fact, I have none stocked. I'm sorry, young lady—I would honor good Gold's request, but I cannot."

"But why can't you get any more from the mines?"

"A golem, child. It appeared at the cave, and not a one can get past it."

A golem: an inorganic monster made from soil and rock, sometimes iron and ore, or stranger things. "Is someone going to slay it? What do you know?"

"Not much. Adventurers have left, but I know no more than that."

Was it that strong? Well, if the golem itself was made of iron, I could see how it would be.

"I'm a blacksmith, young lady," he said, as if reading my mind. "That's all I know. The adventurers' guild may be able to tell you more, if you're curious."

True. Ugh, I was really being given the runaround.

"Yuna," said Fina, "you don't need to overdo it. The knife—"

"Fina, we just went through an interdimensional rift and I got mistaken for an elf *and* we had to find a blacksmith. I am. Going. To buy. The knife. For you. Period, end of story."

You gotta buy something when you want it, whether it's books or merch or whatever. Impulse buys are just more fun. Plus, I don't care if it's a legendary video game mount or a literal real knife for a small child: The harder something is to obtain, the more you want it. And I was nuts for this knife.

But, not really nuts for a mine adventure. I wanted a knife, not to beat up a golem. "Uhh, I know it's odd for me to ask you this, but do the other blacksmiths in the capital not have mithril either?"

"They might, but I doubt they would sell it to a stranger."

I couldn't get mithril in Crimonia and the capital was a no-go too. If I was gonna make that mithril mine, I was gonna make the mine monsters a myth. (Mainly by murdering 'em.) I had to head to the adventurers' guild no matter what.

I thanked Ghazal and left the shop.

147
The Bear Goes to the Adventurers' Guild

AND SO I ENDED UP heading back to that wide thoroughfare—the adventurers' guild was on the same road as the trade guild. If I'd known the troubles I was going to face, I would've just gone to the adventurers' guild to start with, but hindsight is twenty-twenty.

"Um, could you wait here, Fina?" I asked when we got to the front of the guild. I remembered getting in a fight with other adventurers when I'd come to the guild before. I doubted any adventurers would try anything if I had a kid like Fina with me, but you never knew.

"I'm okay. I can go with you. And I actually don't know about being alone..."

Hmm. Several groups of adventurers *were* eyeing us. All right, leaving Fina behind was more anxiety-inducing. I took Fina inside. Whatever happened, Fina was my priority.

Gazes piled up. The reactions were mixed. Some folks knew me, and some didn't.

"What's that?"

"A bear just walked in here."

"Is that the bear from the rumors?"

"What? What rumors?"

"Pssh. You don't know?"

"They're rumors, but I hear there's somethin' to 'em."

(There was some shuddering. I'll admit it: it was pretty nice to see.)

"Why're you terrified of that adorable bear?"

"That's..."

"It's just a normal girl in a cute bear outfit."

"And a kid?"

"Aww! She's cute."

And so on, a whole chorus of buff adventurers in little chairs. Word about me had spread after last time. Fina gripped my bear puppet anxiously.

"So yer saying that's the rumored bear. How about we talk to her?"

"Better not to get yourself involved."

"I don't want a trip to the sky. No, I mean the *literal* sky, man."

"If you're gonna mess with her, you're on your own."

"What's with you? Even you're wussing out?"

"You don't know about the bear warning?"

"The bear warning?"

"Ha! Guy doesn't know about the bear warning. Nah, that girlie is *dangerous*."

"You wanna see the clouds, I'm not stopping you."

A bear warning? Sounded like a sign you'd find in the mountains or something.

You know, it's *still* weird to me that people find a girl wearing a bear onesie so dangerous. Okay, yeah, I had given the adventurers who tried to mess with me a trip to the sky, but—they'd tried to pick a fight with me! They had it coming, you know?

"Do *not* mess with her. The adventurers that messed with her in the past? Dead."

"I'm pretty sure I heard they got eaten."

"Nah, nah. She *minced* them. Alive. Helmut says she did it with a cheese-grater. Rusty one, too."

"That don't mean she didn't eat 'em, too, ya fool."

Uh? All I did was set them up for a cordless bungee jump, I hadn't...hmm. Maybe the stuff from Crimonia was mixed up in there?

There'd been an adventurer who had called me "bloody bear," hadn't there? So maybe the Deboranay incident had gotten mixed up with all that. I'd beaten Deboranay's face swollen, so maybe over time that had turned into me making him mincemeat? Or maybe the rumor was that the adventurers had been smushed when I gave them a taste of cordless bungee jumping?

Either way, they were just rumors. And why was I eating people? I wasn't a literal bear. Why would I bother to put my mouth on some crusty adventurer?

Still, this was way too much commotion just because I'd come here in a bear onesie. At this rate, I wouldn't be able to ask about the mines without hassle. While I was wondering what to do, a back door opened and a woman came out, one with light-green hair—and long ears.

"You're being too loud," she snapped. "Please keep it down." Her name was Sanya. She was the capital's adventurers' guild master and an elf. She'd really helped me out during the king's birthday celebration.

Being the guild master, nobody wanted to mess with her. "What has gotten into you lot?" she asked, looking around the guild. "I'm doing work here. If you keep up the racket, I'll throw you out, and—Yuna?"

"Uh, it's nice to see you again," I said sheepishly.

"What are you doing here? Did you come for work? And that girl there—she was with you before, yes? Fina?"

Fina bobbed her head slightly. I was impressed Sanya remembered her after only meeting her once. I don't think I would've.

286

"I see," she said. "So you're the source of the commotion."

That seemed a little blamey, but okay? Jeez, all I did was come into the guild. I wasn't like, the root of all evil or something. Sure, the bear onesie had *maybe* caused the teensiest bit of ruckus, but what had I done? Nothing. This time.

"Don't make such a fuss about a girl in a bear outfit walking in," Sanya roared.

"But guild master..." one of them whimpered.

"People are saying a ton of things about her," another protested.

I almost wanted to know what those people were saying, but...

"It's true," said Sanya in a commanding voice, "that the adventurers who picked a fight with that bear girl were sent flying through the air. And it's true they were accomplished adventurers. And it is *true* that I happen to be her acquaintance. So please, for all of our sakes, don't throw a little panic party every time she comes in. Consider that an order from your guild master. And please know that if you bother her, you may have to deal with someone even more frightening than me. By which I mean that you will. By which I mean that I could not help you, nor would I bother trying."

Jeez, Sanya went off on the adventurers like a true

guild master, but... Who was supposed to be more frightening then Sanya? She didn't mean the king, did she? If so, things would *really* pop off.

Sanya turned to me now. "So, Yuna, what's up? Did you want work?"

"I came here to ask the guild something...before all this happened." I looked around the room. Asking about the mines wasn't my top priority anymore—things had only barely settled down.

"Ah. Then you can ask me." Sanya looked out at the murmuring adventurers and sighed. "Both of you, come with me." She led us behind the front desk.

The guild master's office was as spacious as I expected. There was a hefty desk by the window in the back and bookshelves laden with all kinds of documents lined the walls. There was a table at the center of the room and chairs sandwiching it. It looked a little like a conference room. Instead of taking her own seat at the back, Sanya sat down in one of the guest chairs in the middle of the room. She looked at us for a moment before urging us down.

"Any seat you like," she said. Fina and I took the ones closest. "What was it that you wanted to ask the guild?"

Finally. I told her everything.

"A mithril knife," she said slowly, rubbing her temple.

"You need a mithril knife...for this child to harvest the black tiger...that you killed protecting the students, who..." Sanya shook her head. "Well, fine. I suppose if you need to harvest a black tiger, you really can't do it with a regular knife. And you came all the way here to the capital for that?"

Yep—and she didn't know about the bear transport gate either, so here I was again looking *really* weird. Ah, well. "I heard from the blacksmith that a golem appeared in the mines."

"Yes, it did. According to the miners who witnessed it, they dug into a giant cavern and awoke the golem inside of it. They all escaped, but barely."

"And now that golem is going wild in the mines?" If it was just one, I felt like an adventurer should be able to defeat it like normal, or at least block it off from the mine proper. Weren't there tons of ways to deal with it?

"It is. It attacks anyone who ventures into the mines, but at least it never leaves."

Kinda reminded me of a dungeon-crawler game. Monsters never left dungeons in those things... Or maybe the golem was protecting something? In games and novels, golems tended to appear as guardians.

"Haven't adventurers gone to slay it?"

"Several have tried, but..." Sanya paused. Sighed. "It

seems to be a difficult one. Apparently, there isn't just one golem."

"Are there multiple?"

"Of this we are sure. Multiple golems have been defeated, yet there are still more. We don't know how many."

Maybe the golems were infinitely spawning? In the game, I would've loved to get some XP grinding them, but when infinite respawn occurred in real life, it was just a nuisance. Oh, and trouble for all the people living nearby, of course.

"On top of that, the normal golems give way to iron golems deep within the cavern. Much more difficult."

Yeah, I guess it'd be a pain to fight one of those in a cave. You couldn't really use elemental fire magic in there, and you couldn't rely on physical earth magic either. As for wind magic, would that even cut through iron? Using water was out of the question, and ice would run into the same issue as earth magic. Really made you wish you had a mithril sword, but... I mean, that was kind of the problem, you know? Ugh.

"So...if I were to go to the mines, would I be able to get my hands on mithril ore?" *Eyes on the mithril, Yuna, not the golems.*

"Hmm, I'm not sure. That would be in the trade guild's jurisdiction."

Oh, come on. I had to go to the trade guild now? Was I just running in circles?

What was going on here? Maybe it'd be better if I gave up on this for a little while? It wasn't like I was in a big hurry to get the black tiger harvested. Also, since I had the bear transport gate, I could come to the capital whenever I wanted. Maybe it'd be best for me to come back when the golem slaying was over.

Ah well. I hadn't been able to get the mithril even after coming all the way out to the capital. Not much I could do about it this time. "Fina, let's give up on this for now. We can have a look around the capital, then go home."

Yep, that was that. We were done. This was over.

But the moment I stood up from my seat, there was a knock at the door.

"Come in." Sanya answered...and indeed, someone came in.

"Huh? Is that you, Yuna and Fina?"

"Ellelaura?!"

Ellelaura, Noa and Shia's mother, entered the room.

KUMA
KUMA
KUMA
BEAR

148
The Bear Is Asked to Defeat the Golem

ELLELAURA LOOKED FLOORED. "Why are you two here?"

Stole the words right out of my mouth. "Ellelaura, why are you at the adventurers' guild?"

"I had business with Sanya."

"Well, *I* had something I wanted to ask the guild."

Ellelaura came over to us and sat down next to Fina, who ended up sandwiched between us. "Fina. Are you well? Eating your vegetables?"

"Um. Yes."

"Is Noa doing all right?"

"Yes, we played together the other day."

I'd occasionally seen the two of them together. Sometimes they came to the bear house and played with

Kumayuru and Kumakyu. It looked like they were getting along.

"I hope you'll keep playing with her in the future too," said Ellelaura.

"I will," said Fina with a smile.

"Now, Lady Ellelaura," said Sanya, "what brings you here?"

"I wanted to ask about that issue from earlier."

"You're referring to the mines?"

"I am. Leaving the mines as they are now would be an issue for the country, so I was considering dispatching the soldiers to deal with it."

"Well, there are C-Rank adventurers headed there now."

"How many?"

"Two parties of four and five people."

"Hmm. So we wait, then? I suppose if they fail, we will...cope with it."

Why *not* send out soldiers, knights, or mages? It'd get settled quicker, and I'd finally get my hands on mithril.

When I asked, they gave me the rundown. As a rule, monster appearances were the adventurers' guild's job to deal with. If the national soldiers dealt with everything, there wouldn't be work for adventurers.

As long as it wasn't an emergency, the country wouldn't act to back them up. This was the unspoken agreement between the adventurers' guild and the country, and it was why the guild had to try their hand first. If that didn't work, only then the country would mobilize. It was a pain, but that was just how things rolled.

Plus, the country's soldiers might be needed to deal with other stuff elsewhere. What would happen if another country invaded and the soldiers were dealing with a golem in some cave?

"Why are you here, Yuna?" asked Ellelaura, and I did the exposition thing for the millionth time. "The mithril, huh?" Ellelaura looked at me with an odd grin. I was getting a bad feeling about this. "Then perhaps you could do something for me. If I get any mithril, I'll prioritize sending it to you in an...exchange."

"Let me guess: You want me to slay the golems?" Naturally.

"Oh, there's a C-Rank party there. I'm sure things will be fine, but...I'd like a powerful adventurer like you there as well. Just in case."

"Why me? I want mithril, sure, but you could ask another high-ranking adventurer instead." I hadn't seen an adventurer in B-Rank or above yet. But there had to be some in the capital, right?

"It's a little difficult to ask them to do quests."

"Huh?" I tilted my head to the side.

"Well, first, high-ranking adventurers tend to have quite a bit of wanderlust. They like going to wildlands and searching for strong monsters, so we never know when they'll come back, let alone where they currently are. As for stronger mages, they very rarely come out of their homes once they've shut themselves away to research magic. Adventurers as a whole tend to be odd people, so any requests can be difficult."

Odd people. Both Sanya and Ellelaura gave me a look at that. That didn't seem fair, why would—and *then* I noticed that even Fina was giving me a look. Come on, this was gonna bum me out. I wasn't odd. I was just a bear, you know?

"Another reason." Ellelaura continued, "is that there simply aren't many high-rank adventurers."

That made sense—maybe that was why I hadn't met one yet. Then again, I hadn't been going to the adventurers' guild super often, and hadn't really asked about any other adventurers. Maybe that was why I just hadn't seen any.

"Even if there were one available," Sanya threw in, "the high-ranking adventurers have ample funds, so they rarely need to take work, and so they don't."

Wait.

Hold on.

This all sounded like *me*.

I had money, so I fundamentally didn't want to work. I wanted to see the world, so I also wanted to go on adventures. Researching novel magic seemed like fun. I didn't want to do it to figure out how strong I was, but I did want to see how powerful my bear gear could be. When I thought of it that way, I could understand how these high-ranking adventurers felt.

But that was just me, personally. I mean, anybody normal would feel like that. Right? Right.

"So Yuna...would you kindly take the quest?"

I *did* want mithril, so...I supposed I could accept. The only issue was those golems.

A normal golem made from earth or rock was one thing, but I didn't know if I could defeat an iron golem. As I brooded over it, I noticed someone tugging on my bear clothes. "Fina?"

Fina shook her head slightly. "Yuna, it's dangerous. I don't need a mithril knife, so please don't put yourself in danger. You can just ask the guild to harvest the black tiger."

She said she didn't need it, but...I wanted it even more now. Plus, who knew when we would *really* need mithril? "It'll be fine. You know I'm strong, don't you?" I plunked my bear puppet onto Fina's head. "I accept your quest."

"Thank you, Yuna. You're a lifesaver. Well then, I'll take Fina to my house while you're out."

"Huh?" Fina and I gaped.

Ellelaura looked shocked. "You weren't planning on taking her with you, were you?" she said, giving Fina a hug. I wasn't, but I supposed I couldn't just say that I was taking her back to Crimonia either.

"Please take care of her," I said.

"Yuna?!" Fina also looked shocked when I said that. I mean, it wasn't like I could talk about the bear transport gate, and I definitely couldn't take her with me. Leaving her alone in the capital was right out. What other choice did I have?

"I'll be back before you know it."

"But my mom..."

"It'll be fine." I just needed to stop by Crimonia real quick and ask Tiermina for permission to borrow Fina. It'd be a problem if she said no, but I bet that things would work out as long as I asked.

I told Sanya and Ellelaura I had to get some things at my house in the capital, used the bear transport gate to go to Crimonia, and asked Tiermina for permission to borrow Fina for a few days. Tiermina happily agreed, thankfully. Once I got that squared, I headed back to

the capital through the bear transport gate and ended up having to go through the pains of leaving Fina with Ellelaura.

"Ugh, why did things end up like this?" Fina groaned. She looked pretty miserable about it all, staying at the aristocrat Ellelaura's mansion.

"Oh, I have some clothes that would look simply adorable on Fina."

"C'mon, she's not a doll. Don't be mean."

"I've never been mean in my entire life. I'll strive to take excellent care of her. And I must thank her, as it seems that she's been getting along well with Noa."

"But it's Lady Noa who's been taking care of *me*."

"Nonsense. I can't thank your family, so you'll just need to accept my gratitude."

Fina gave me a miserable look. "Yunaaaaaaa..."

C'mon, she was gonna make me miserable too! "I'll be back before you know it."

"Yuna, please come back soon."

I prayed that Fina wouldn't get too distressed. I mean, I'd be back soon, so she just had to wait for a little while.

And so I headed off on my solo journey to the mines to slay the golem and return to save the captured princess.

Wait, what? How had I ended up doing *this*?

Ehh, whatever. It was golem-slaying time.

The Bear Makes Bear Bread with Mil
Part One

HI! My name is Mil, I'm twelve, and I'm one of the girls working at Yuna's bakery.

It's been a while since Yuna came to the orphanage. She's cool. Yuna gave me work looking after birds, warm food and clothes, and a room (that's right, a *room)*. On top of that, since she was opening a bakery, she said she wanted help.

Apparently, she wanted kids who could read and write and do math. And guess what? I could do all that. Even better, she *really* wanted kids who liked cooking. I raised my hand.

"I want to do it."

Before I knew it, there were six kids plus me, and we were going to work at the bakery. First, she introduced us to Morin, who was the lady who was gonna teach us how to make bread. She had a daughter named Karin.

Morin was super strict but real kind. Karin was real cheerful, even if she was older than us. First Karin taught us how to make bread, but she also taught us how to serve customers, how to say hi to them, how to deal with money, clean, and more. If we didn't learn how to do those things right, it would be really bad, she said, and the customers would walk away. If we got the cost of the bread wrong, then someone would lose money. If the shop was dirty, then the customers would just not come anymore! We learned all kinds of things from Karin that were important for the shop. Morin smiled from the side while we did. I wonder why?

The day the shop opened, pudding, bread, and pizza orders came in like a big ol' thunderstorm rain. It was tough. Karin gave us directions so we wouldn't get mixed up. I dunno what we'd have done without her. It would've been messy.

"Wipe down the table by the running bear."

"Yes, ma'am!"

"Clean up the table with the sleeping bear."

Karin used the bears decorating the tops of the tables

for her directions. That was real smart, and it helped us go fast—you could remember which bear was on what table easy. Since lunchtime was the busiest, things got less crazy in the afternoon.

I was way happy for the bread and pudding we made, cuz it sold great! The pudding we made from the eggs was even more popular. I thought it was a little expensive, or maybe even very, very, *very* expensive. Tiermina said it was a fair price, but we were getting a lot of money. It was kinda like a dream to see that much money in real life?

Tiermina said it would be good for the orphanage to have it. This money would turn into warm meals and warm clothes, which seemed crazy, but I didn't think she meant it would *really* do that, because she wouldn't say something like that. Anyway, I didn't want to go back to how we were before Yuna came, so I worked real hard, as hard as I could.

When we worked at the shop, we would wear bear out-fits. They were real cute! It made me kinda happy since I would look like Yuna. But Karin apparently wouldn't wear one because she said it was embarrassing.

(I hope nobody tells her, but I don't get that at all.)

The customers liked these bear outfits too! They would always tell us that we were cute. Maybe it was a *little* embarrassing, but it made me happy. Isn't that the important part?

We finished things one day, and the next one was gonna be our day off.

After every six days of work, we got one free day. It's way important to rest, everyone says, and I say so too! We could do anything when we had a break. I did a lot of things, like help with work at the orphanage. That day there was a new bread I wanted to make, so I went to a shop.

When I went there, Karin was already making bread. On days off, Karin would bake for the orphanage. It was for practice, apparently. "Mil, why are you here?"

"There was some bread I wanted to make real quick."

The other day, I'd brought back bread to the orphanage. I'd made it myself. Everyone at the orphanage would eat the extra bread and the practice bread. Once, one of the small girls at the orphanage asked me something. "Isn't there any bear bread?"

When I asked her what she meant, she told me she meant bread shaped like a bear. Since she was still small, she had apparently combined the Bear's Lounge name with being a bakery and thought that we made bear bread.

So...I went to the shop to make bear bread! I put on my bear uniform and got ready to make it.

First, I kneaded the dough. Then I made it into a bear shape. I did it like this: I made the legs, made the arms, and made a round, poofy tail. I couldn't make a good face. It didn't look much like a bear. Maybe an animal, but not a bear...

I went to look at the bear ornaments inside the shop.

They were very cute bears! According to Yuna, making something scary like this cute was called "cartoonifying"? Let's see, how could you make a bear cute? I looked carefully at one and shaped the bear bread on a nearby table, but...nope. No matter how much I tried to copy the ornament, the bread didn't look good.

I was fighting really hard to get it right when someone called out to me. "Mil, what are you doing?"

When I looked up, I saw Yuna!

When I told her what I was doing, she looked at my hands. I felt a little embarrassed. "I was copying this bear to make bear bread."

"Bear what?" Yuna looked real curious.

"Someone at the orphanage said she wanted to eat bear bread, so I tried making it! But I can't make it look as nice as the bears you made."

When I told her that, Yuna looked at the bear bread I

had made. It kinda made me feel bad, because it looked so wrong. "Um, please don't look too close."

"Is it the body that's hard?"

"Mmhm. And the face too. That's harder."

Actually, out of all of it, the face was hardest. When I looked at Yuna... Oh, no... She looked sad, or like she was thinking real hard. Was my bear bread that bad?

"You're not making this for the shop, are you?" she asked.

"No, I wanted to make it for the other kids to eat."

"You really mean that?"

For some reason, she asked a few more times in different ways. I nodded. I didn't really understand, but Yuna looked like she had made up her mind.

"Could you let me borrow the dough for a bit?" she asked.

"Uh-huh!"

I let her have two different colored doughs, and she started to knead them each lightly. I'd prepped them thinking that the white dough could look like Kumakyu and the brown dough could look like Kumayuru. Yuna rounded out the brown dough into a ball and flattened it slightly to make a disk. She put new, small pieces of dough on the disk and put some of the white dough on it to form the shape of the bread.

Now that she had gotten this far, I understood what she was doing too.

"It's a bear's face!"

Yuna had made a bear face. Yuna's hands were almost exactly like Morin's...it was like magic!

"Bake it like this, and it'll be done," she said. "It's easier to make just the face versus the whole body, right?"

Yeah, I could tell it was a bear just by looking at the face. And it looked so easy. It looked like something I could make too. "Could I try?"

"Go for it."

I copied Yuna and kneaded the dough. I made two bear faces with it. They looked a little different from Yuna's, but I could do it!

"There we go! Let's fire these up, eh?"

"Yeah!"

We borrowed the stone oven Karin was using to bake bread.

"What did you make?" she asked us.

Yuna shook her head gravely. I nodded. "It's a secret until it's done baking," I told Karin.

I was so excited to see it baked that I waited in front of the oven. It was hot, but I beared with it. I could see it rising.

Once we pulled the bread out of the oven, the bear

bread was done. Karin peeked at it. "Looks like a bear face. You did a great job. I think the right one is a little better though."

"Yuna made the right one. I made the left one."

"No worries, Mil," said Karin. "Once you practice, you'll get better. Everyone starts as a beginner."

Jeez. Just watching Yuna, I felt like she could do anything. Was there anything she couldn't do? I wanted to be more like her!

"Well, how about we taste test these?" Yuna asked.

"Okay."

It felt kind of like a waste to eat them, even if they were just normal bread. But Yuna didn't seem bothered, and she pulled off one of the bear's ears. I felt kind of bad for the poor bear bread.

"Can I try some too?" asked Karin. She tore off some of Yuna's and took a bite. "Looks like it's baked through."

"Huh. You know, we could put something in this," said Yuna.

That did sound pretty yummy...

"You're not going to have some, Mil?" Yuna asked me.

I kept holding the bear, but... "I feel like it's kind of a waste."

"Ehh. I get it, but it'd *really* be a waste to let it go un-eaten. You should at least try it."

Yeah! I needed to make sure it tasted good. I also tore off a bear ear and ate it. It was delicious. But now the bear was missing an ear.

A little sad, but definitely tasty!

Then Karin joined in and we thought about what we could use to fill the bread and what flavors to use, and we made all kinds of bear bread. We made a few mistakes, but they all were delicious mistakes! I knew they'd be glad to eat 'em.

Then I brought our efforts home to the orphanage. The super little kids picked up the bread in their tiny hands. But the bear bread was so big and difficult to eat that I had to split the heads in half in front of them, which made them start crying.

"The bear!" All of them just wouldn't stop crying. I said sorry again and again. Since we'd broken them in half when we were testing them—I mean Yuna and Karin and me—I was used to just doing that without thinking. I felt sad back then, too, but it was so yummy I'd forgotten!

I pulled out a new bear bread for them. They spent an eternity treating the bread like it was very important, but they had to eat it at some point. The little kids apologized to the bears real seriously ("I'm sorry, bear") before they ate it.

A few days later, we started to lay out bear bread in the shop. When Yuna saw that, she looked like she wasn't sure about something. I wonder why?

The Bear Makes Bear Bread with Mil
Part Two

IT WAS A DAY OFF at the Bear's Lounge, and this particular bear (I mean, Yuna) was feeling a little peckish. Chalk that up to the smell of bread wafting from the back. Someone was baking, and I had to at least ask if I could have some. Just in case.

When I headed into the kitchen from the back entrance, Karin was baking bread. Sometimes she'd practice baking on days off, asking orphans for their opinions, and use their input to improve her stuff.

"Morning, Karin. Can I have some bread?"

"Yuna? Take as much as you'd like."

I reached out for the bread Karin had baked and ate some. Yup, scrumptious. What else could I expect from Morin's daughter?

"Just you today, Karin?"

"My mom is out, so yup. Oh, Mil is here too though."

"Mil?"

"Yeah, she said she wanted to make something and headed to the main floor."

That piqued my curiosity, so I headed over to check out what was up. Then I heard Mil saying stuff like, "I can't do it," and, "This is hard."

"Mil, what are you doing?"

When I asked her that, she told me she was making bread. Under her hands was a loaf that looked like some kind of animal shape. Apparently, she'd been trying to use the Nendoroid-esque bear decorations on the table as a model to make bread.

When I asked her why, she told me the orphans wanted "bear bread." That was why Mil was trying to copy the bears I'd made. The face was apparently too difficult, and she was in a tight spot.

I wanted to help her out, but, uh, she was making bread in the shape of a bear. I *could* have asked why, but it was pretty obvious: It was all because of me, as usual.

"You're not making this for the shop, are you?" I asked.

"No, I wanted to make it for the other kids to eat."

"You really mean that?"

She said she was bringing it to the orphanage. She

wasn't making it to sell at the shop, so...you know what? Sure, why not. I got multiple colors of dough from Mil and started making a bear face. Making a whole body would be difficult, but a face was easy enough. I'd seen a lot of bread of just bear faces in my old world.

Aaaaand there it was. It looked about right. Mil sure seemed to think so, from her expression. The face was a little off-center, but it was my first try, so that was just how it be. It looked bearish enough.

"You're amazing, Yuna! It's a bear face."

That it was. Good job, kid. And hey, she wanted to copy it too! She used her small hands to make her own while consulting my bread as a model.

"I'm done."

It looked like a perfectly good bear face to me. "Let's fire these up, eh?"

Mil and I headed back to the kitchen, borrowed the stone oven from Karin, and baked the doughy little dudes. Mil wouldn't budge from in front of the oven.

"Yuna, what did you make?"

I looked to Mil—she seemed pretty psyched about it, so I shook my head and said to Karin in my most serious adult voice: "It's a secret until it's done."

"Looks like it's baked through," said Karin, and Mil brought over the finished bear bread with a smile on her face. They looked way better than I'd thought—the bear heads were even the right color.

Karin peeked at them from the side. "Looks like bear bread. You did a great job. I think the right one is a little better though."

"Yuna made the right one. I made the left one," Mil answered, seeming embarrassed.

"No worries, Mil. Once you practice, you'll get better at it. Everyone starts as a beginner," said Karin.

After we tasted the bread, Karin started helping us make more bear bread. We made all different kinds for the orphans, and Mil took them back to the orphanage with her. She kept bubbling over about how happy she was to give them the bread she had baked. You know, I was pretty happy too.

The next day, when I asked Mil how the kids reacted, she looked like she wasn't sure about something? Weird. Had something gone wrong?

Then, after a while, the shop started selling bear bread. I wonder why?

EXTRA STORY

The Bear Accompanies the Novice Adventurers' Practice

I'D MADE A PROMISE, so it was time to meet up again with Horn. I'd seen her the day before at the Bear's Lounge and she'd asked me to take a look at her magic. Well, I was curious about whether she had been practicing and improving, so why not?

We promised to meet in the same spot as last time. There was nothing of note there, so it wouldn't cause any trouble...but I was still in for a surprise.

There was a random dude. A, uh...oh, yeah, his name was...J...Jhin? And they were in the same party.

Horn waved. "See, Shin? She's here!"

And by Jhin I obviously meant Shin, which was pretty much almost kind of the basically same thing, if you thought about it. Philosophically. But what was he doing here? Maybe he'd come because he was worried I was bullying Horn? I was apparently the bloody bear, if you asked around. I couldn't blame anybody for being freaked if they thought there was truth to the rumor.

"Ms. Yuna," she said, "thank you for coming."

"It was a promise, wasn't it? So, what's he doing here? He's part of your party, isn't he, Horn?"

"C'mon, Shin."

Horn pushed J—that is, pushed Shin's back. "Um," he said, "can I observe?"

"The magic?"

"Yeah, Horn's gotten really good at magic, so I wanted to know how you were teaching her. If it's a secret, I can head home."

"I don't mind. I'm not teaching anything significant." My pedagogy was to go with the flow, man. I had no idea if I was doing it right. I was just teaching the way I'd learned it, and it was working out well enough.

I created a small, reinforced mound about a meter high a slight distance away using earth magic, giving Horn something to test herself on.

"Well, then," I said, walking back up to her, "let's check your progress. Try some magic on that dirt pile. Go wild."

"Okay."

Horn called up her earth magic. She created an earth clod about as big as a baseball in front of her. She made it spin at high speed and sent it flying at the dirt pile. The earth clod sunk straight into the pile of dirt. I could even see the tracks it left behind.

Yeah, she'd really built up the power on that baby. Good on her.

"Thanks to you," she said happily, "I don't hold everyone back now." She looked like she was about to jump up and down, which would've—actually, I guess we were pretty much in the middle of nowhere, so I supposed that wouldn't cause any kind of scene.

"In that case," I said, "I'll teach you something practical. If you can do this, I think you can beat some real monsters."

"Do you really think so?"

"Sure. Not that it'll be easy, mind you." I created a thin pole from earth. It was pointed at the end. It wasn't exactly an arrow so much as a thin, short spear. I made that short spear rotate really fast. Then, when I let it loose, it pierced the small dirt mountain and left a tiny hole.

Horn's jaw dropped. "Whoa."

"That's amazing," whispered Shin.

"She's all yours," I said.

"Um." Horn stood in front of the dirt pile. "Okay."

Readied herself. "Make a thin pole. That's first. Then I... yeah, I make the tip pointed like an arrow."

Thin pole, check. Sharpened point, done.

"Then I make it spin," she said. Took a breath. "And, um. Okay. Then...then I shoot it."

Spin, spin, aaaaaand...whump-crack. It hit the dirt mound, but the earth spear shattered.

"Is it the spin?"

"Nah. It's not strong enough. You need to make it as hard as the ball."

"But it's so thin. I can't imagine it being so...I don't know, so dense? When it's a ball, I can see it all in my head, like the dirt is pressing into its center. I don't know how to think of it, when it's a pole."

I shrugged. "Horn, I mean this in a nice way, but that is a *you* problem. And *you* can practice that, because I've seen you do just that. Get it dense, get it spinning, hit those monsters where it hurts, and I know you'll up your power in battle."

"Would I be able to stop an orc?"

"An orc?"

"We were doing some slaying around the Bear Tunnel earlier. When we did that, an orc attacked us, and we were nearly goners."

Oh, um. Dealing with an orc myself was one thing,

but…thinking about Horn and her friends was…yeah, that was different. "You're okay, right? All of you are okay?"

In Japan, death felt really far away. But…"nearly goners"? I had my onesie to protect me now, and I'd had a cushy life back home. This was different. This kinda scared me.

"Yes, some adventurers named Rulina and Gil helped us when we were in trouble," Horn said.

"Gil was so cool," added Shin.

Whew. Okay. Exhale, Yuna: Rulina and Gil had saved them. It's fine, and really not even a big deal. In fact, come to think of it, I think Rulina had mentioned participating in some monster slaying near the Bear Tunnel.

"You know Rulina, don't you, Yuna?" asked Horn.

"Well, we *are* adventurers." I'd suffered the big dumb attack from Deboranay, accepted a quest with Rulina, and eventually asked her to guard the shop that one time. We were less close and more occasional coworkers.

"If we could have just defeated that orc…" said Horn, almost to herself. "No, if we just could have stopped it back then, I think we could have run away."

It was weird, thinking of an orc like that. I could whack an orc in one hit. However strong an orc was to anyone who qualified as baseline normal, I couldn't internalize that differential. Even when I used the same magic as somebody else, our abilities were totally different. Our mana was different, too—the same magic could wildly differ depending on how much mana you had inside of you.

"You're talking about defeating that orc, Horn, but... when I say that's a you problem, I really do mean that. If you don't practice, you'll stay the Horn you are. That's fine, if you want, but I don't think you *do* want it. That Horn, that girl you are right now...maybe she could take one on, and maybe not. The only way you'll ever know is to try. Otherwise, you're just this Horn right here. And she's all right. I like her. But I don't know if that's who you wanna be."

There was no other way I could respond. She had to actually try to know for sure. That whole greeting card junk about anybody being able to do anything...if you say that to somebody and they can't do a thing, what happens then? That's pretty irresponsible, right? Nah, I wouldn't say anything haphazardly.

But hey, it looked like it had worked pretty well: She seemed motivated!

Horn started to really apply herself to practicing. She cast her magic and fired it off at the dirt pile time after time.

"You don't have to be in a hurry, though," I said. "Think about the strength of it, how fast you're spinning it, and how much mana you're putting into it. Each thing, *think* about it."

"Okay." Horn took a deep breath and then slowly started to cast her magic.

While I was watching Horn practice from a short distance away, Shin spoke up. "Hey, why're you just teaching her like this? There's nothing we can give to thank you."

"Hey, I don't know. I don't really *want* anything, you know?"

"Then why are you teaching her?"

"Because she's Horn. You know, Horn? Over there? Your friend? If she ended up dead because I was greedy and didn't wanna teach her, what kind of person would I be? I'd feel like a heel forever."

"But you just met us."

"Sure, I guess. If Horn had mocked me and been a mean kid, I think I wouldn't have taught her. And I wouldn't have been too broken up if she wound up on the wrong end of an orc sword or something. But Horn's all right. Why wouldn't I help her?"

We'd talked. I didn't want her to die. Why was this so complicated?

"Um..." Shin shuffled his feet, oddly embarrassed. "Thanks for teaching her."

"Long as you don't hold her back, man." She'd grown

since I first met her. I had no idea how powerful she'd become, but who knew if guys like this were going to be footnotes in her story?

"I know that," he said. "Gil taught me a whole bunch of stuff earlier, so I'm in the middle of intensive training."

"You are?"

I was curious, so I asked what Gil had taught him: Put on some muscle, he'd said. Build up stamina, watch your opponent. Learn some techniques through experience. If you still can't win after that, rely on your teammates. Stuff like that. He'd taught them the basics right.

"So I've been running and swinging my sword to gain some stamina and muscle."

"Then…" I was getting a little bored. "…You want to have a quick match with me?" If Horn was gonna make it as an adventurer, the people around her needed to toughen up too. How strong was this Shin guy, really?

"A match with you? But aren't you a mage?"

"I'm whatever I gotta be." I pulled my tree branch from my bear storage, broke it off at a random point to make a one-meter-long branch. I made wind magic swirl around the two branches, whittling them down with a high whipping crack until I created two round, easy-to-grip practice swords. I threw one over to Shin. He took it, though he seemed surprised.

"I won't use magic," I said. "Come at me however you like."

"Are you really sure? I'm not gonna hold back. Don't come crying to me if you get hurt."

Shin gripped the branch and brandished it at me.

I lightly caught the blow.

We had a cute little match.

Shin lay panting on the ground, an exhausted heap. The results were in: Turned out he was weak. What a surprise. Not that I really knew what *strong* was supposed to mean, but I sure knew the alternative.

"H-how were you able to move that fast, Yuna?"

I wasn't even out of breath. "I have training methods that some might find...unusual."

Which was a pretty nice way of saying "I'd never trained in my whole life." Still, even though my physical strength was a sham, I'd learned my techniques through the game. That...was a *kind* of training, right? From a certain point of view?

"There was," I added, "*something* I noticed. You wanna hear?"

"Damn it." He kind of seemed upset.

"Well? Do you?"

"Pl-please give me your advice." Shin dropped his head.

"Then here you go: Don't waste all that effort swinging your sword so hard. When you're easing off, you gotta *really* ease off."

"But you're supposed to swing your sword hard, right?"

"Not if you wanna maintain your grip. If you're always gripping something hard, that grip's gonna weaken. If you go at it too long, you won't be able to hold your sword. If you keep waving your sword around when you don't need to, you'll get so tired you won't be able to do much of anything. It's the same with running—you'll lose your stamina."

"But that's *why* I'm running and building up muscle! That's what Gil said, at least."

"And can you hold a heavy sword like Gil? Swing it like him?" If Gil was a hundred, Shin was a ten. They weren't in the same ballpark—weren't in the same *city*.

"But...if I work hard enough, then..."

"Maybe then, yeah, but getting stronger takes time. Even if you work hard, your body's gonna be different in little ways. Everybody's is."

He slumped. "So what do I do?"

"Start thinking about technique."

"Technique? Um, I never got taught, so I don't know what you mean. I guess there *is* that thing Gil said about watching the enemy. Where am I supposed to look?"

"Where are you looking when you fight?"

Shin frowned thoughtfully. "I guess...their weapon?"

He wasn't wrong, exactly, but... "You're supposed to look at everything."

"Everything?"

"The weapon's a start, but what about the hand that holds it? What foot are they stepping forward with? Where are *they* looking, how are *they* breathing? And if they outclass you, you've got to really get in tune with your environment."

"Do you do all that?"

"More or less. If they move their foot, I can predict their timing. If I look at the hand gripping a sword, I can tell how much effort they're putting into it. If I track their gaze, I can tell what they're targeting. Just one of these details doesn't give you the whole picture; you've got to put it all together to figure out what they're gonna do. You can't predict everything, but it's a start...and remember that as you watch an enemy, they're watching you too."

If you zeroed in on only one spot, you could get tunnel vision. If you looked only at someone's weapon, they could get away with other tricks.

"Also," I said, "you said you're not as strong as Gil, right? So learn when to use your strength. When you see an opening, use all the power you got. Waiting itself can be a technique." You didn't need to put a lot of effort into a feint, after all—you just needed to find your moment.

"But that's when you're up against a person, right? What about monsters?"

"That's not so different. Lots of goblins and orcs carry weapons. Wolves have legs, don't they? Watch how they step. And yeah, monsters are often in groups, but when you learn to really see the parts of your opponent, you can turn multiple opponents into parts too."

Which could help you see who was gonna attack, and when. Look at the big picture, and use that to figure out who to go after and which of your companions to protect.

Yeah, I was generally a loner, but I'd known how to run a party in the game.

"Look for someone who doesn't seem like they're doing anything at the adventurers' guild and ask them to practice with you. I'm sure Gil told you the same thing, right? Experience is important. Gaining it in battle is dangerous, but you can learn a lot from practice without risking more than a bruise or two. Or *maybe* a few more."

"All right. I'll try," said Shin, nodding slowly.

Since I was talking to Shin, I wasn't watching Horn, but when I did look, she was still practicing her magic like she was supposed to. She was a diligent student.

I finished off that day taking on Horn and Shin. And sure, there were a few bruises, but no way was I going to let them end up dead.

KUMA
KUMA
KUMA
BEAR

EXTRA STORY
Mileela's Damon

THE SUDDEN ARRIVAL of a kraken in the town of Mileela robbed us of our ability to go out to sea. The only highway to other towns was overrun with bandits, so we couldn't travel along that either. The rich had left.

In a month, the seaport had a food shortage.

After talking with my family, I decided to climb over the Elezent mountain range to buy food in Crimonia. My wife Yuula and I climbed the steep mountain to get there—we heard that it was possible, despite the danger. But as we got closer to the summit, a strong snowstorm obscured our vision until we couldn't see in front of us.

Every single step was a nightmare. We grew numb and couldn't walk. There was nowhere to avoid the storm... and then something fell down behind me. Yuula had collapsed. I shouted to her over the roaring storm, but she didn't move. I tried to carry Yuula on my back, but I was too weak.

My body was at its limit too. I thought of the children. It was no use. Bit by bit, darkness swallowed me.

When I woke up, I was in a warm house with...a girl in a bear outfit? She gave me something warm to drink and something to eat. The food was delicious, and its warmth spread through my shivering body.

All of that was shocking enough, but then I found out the house itself was in the mountain range.

The girl in the bear outfit split her provisions with us. She said that showing her around Mileela would be thanks enough for her, so we ended up going back the way we came down the mountain.

We went down on bears, of all things. Apparently, these were the bear girl's summons. The bears easily clambered down the mountain we toiled so hard to climb. It was downright dreamlike.

After days of mountain climbing, we returned home in less than a day.

All kinds of things happened after the bear girl came to the seaport. Food appeared. The bandits on the highway were subdued. On top of that, the trade guild master was implicated in a plot with the bandits.

We could travel on the highway, so a caravan headed out to buy food. Sure, it would take time, but we had hope. All thanks to the bear girl...

Since there was a kraken in the ocean, I'd been staying at home—no point in a fisherman like me going out, after all—when all the fishers were instructed to gather under old man Kuro's name. Many fishers were already gathered at the rendezvous point by the time I arrived.

Old man Kuro came before us and told us we were to stay at home and not go near the ocean under any circumstances the day after tomorrow.

"What's going on, old man Kuro?" I asked.

"You know what you need to know, lad. Under no conditions are you to approach the ocean on that day, hear me?" We were already avoiding the ocean on account of the kraken, but it was odd for old man Kuro to go out of his way to give us one specific day to *especially* avoid it.

"For better or worse," he continued, "the seaport's fate will be decided then. If the worst happens, I will take responsibility for it. But on that day, do *not* approach the ocean." Stubborn old Kuro bowed his head low, looking pretty serious for a man who had just told us to keep doing the thing we'd already *been* doing.

"Old man Kuro," I said, "we understand, so please raise your head. We have no idea what's going to happen, but we trust you. We'll follow your instructions. Right, everyone?"

"Yes, that's right." We vowed to old man Kuro that we absolutely wouldn't go near the ocean on that day.

Still, I found myself so troubled by old Kuro's words that I couldn't stay cooped up in my house that day, so I went for a walk around the seaport to distract myself.

Even walking around town, I couldn't help but wonder what was happening with the ocean. I didn't have to go *near* it to see what was going on. Just a little closer, and...

Odd. The adventurers' guild staff were standing in front of the seaport exit gate as though they were blocking it. I tried talking to them, but they stonewalled me. "We're not letting anyone through today."

Just what was going on? Did it have to do with old Kuro's warnings?

I tried a few other angles to get a look before, suddenly, a commotion broke out at the gate. At the center of it... was the bear girl, collapsed on her white bear.

What had happened to her? The adventurers' guild master was trying to go in with the bear, but the gate guard seemed troubled about whether to let the bear through.

Huffing and furious, the guild master quietly scolded everyone: She said that the bear girl had defeated the kraken.

Hold on, she'd *defeated the kraken*?

That was ridiculous...right? But she said that the girl had defeated the kraken on a cliff just a little way from here. But the bear girl had used up too much mana fighting the kraken and collapsed.

It couldn't be real. I mean...*could* it?

Well, the guild master told us we'd see it if we headed over. Several men, me included, ran to the cliff to check if our seaport was saved.

When I got to the cliff, panting with exhaustion, a terrific amount of steam rose all around. I was sweating something awful, but where was the steam coming from? I followed it...several gigantic bear statues appeared from the steam, rising from the ocean and surrounding a dead kraken.

I couldn't believe that the girl in such a cute bear outfit could've done this. I mean, people talk about not believing something till you see it with your own eyes, but even seeing it wasn't helping much. Still, the kraken that had tormented us was unmistakably dead in the boiling ocean.

Something rolled down my cheek. Oh, I…I was crying. I hadn't even noticed. Flustered, I wiped away my tears. I wasn't the only one crying, though—the others who ran over with me were sobbing too.

The kraken lay below us, defeated at last.

I headed to Deigha's inn where the girl was staying.

She'd apparently collapsed from exhaustion from her fight with the kraken. The guild master, Atola, asked us to let her rest, since she was sleeping so peacefully right now.

I understood, but I wanted to thank her—we all did—and before long there was a crowd of townspeople gathering around the inn.

Atola and the innkeeper Deigha finally addressed us: "If you want to help, bring rice for her. Even a slight amount would be fine. Out of all food, that one will really make her day."

Murmurs all around, then. "Rice, you say?"

"Will that really make her happy?"

"Yeah, I bet it will. When she wakes up, I'm sure she'll be over the moon."

"Right. Better than making a ruckus and waking her with it."

We all headed home—it sounded reasonable—and I told my family about it. We picked what little rice we had for her (there was nothing else I could offer), and I brought my daughter with me to the inn so we could give her the gift.

There were already several other townspeople there, pouring the rice into a giant barrel that it looked like Deigha had prepped. Limited as our food supplies were, everyone was still eager to bring the girl rice from their limited food supplies.

My daughter poured our rice into the barrel too. "Dad, do you think this will make the bear girl happy?"

"Yeah, I'm sure it will."

She smiled. "Thank you, bear girl." My daughter held my hand and said her thanks. I really wanted to thank the bear girl in person, but this was all I could manage for now.

The girl had battled something so nightmarish, so incredible, that I couldn't even imagine the ordeal. She had probably risked her life in that fight. I mean, I'd seen her collapsed on that white bear.

She deserved a good rest.

The next day, I headed out to the ocean. The sway of the boat, the smell of the sea—it was like coming home.

A smile snuck up on my face—and not just mine. All of us sailors were smiling. It's hard to explain to an outsider, what the ocean means to us.

After I caught fish and headed back, I was asked to come to the nearby beach, since we'd be harvesting the kraken. The bear girl and old man Kuro waited for us there.

The waves had hidden just how massive the kraken was. We ended up splitting the work to harvest it.

I'd heard that the kraken materials were all going to the seaport—the bear girl had done that for us too. No way I'd believe somebody would do that...or I never *used* to think somebody would. She could have asked us for an inordinate amount of money for her deed, but she didn't ask for a thing.

If I weren't here—if any of we townspeople hadn't seen it with our own eyes—I don't know if we'd have believed it.

The girl in the bear outfit really was a mystery.

The townspeople were grateful to her, but things started to get hectic after she saved the seaport. The feudal lord of Crimonia came by: They'd discovered a tunnel connecting us to that town. They said that the bear girl had come across it, but I didn't buy it. If any tunnel like that had existed, she never would've gone out of her way to climb up the Elezent mountain range.

She'd slain the kraken. I wondered what else she might be capable of...

Since the tunnel had been discovered, we were going to have food delivered from Crimonia, but we'd need to secure a route for the carriages to travel along. It was all pretty urgent, so the new trade guild master Jeremo had his work cut out for him.

Heh. It cracked me up, thinking about that dawdler becoming guild master, but...he was an all right guy, all things told. With him serving as guild master, the trade guild would do well for us all.

Now, after all of that, I had business at the trade guild—with Jeremo, specifically.

"Heya, Jeremo! Looks like you're busy."

"Is that you, Damon? Looks like you've got time on your hands."

"Ha! No, I was out working in the ocean today, as usual."

"Sounds like fun. I'd like that."

"If you ever come along, be sure to thank that girl again for opening the waters to us. And now we have so many orders for fish from your trade guild."

Jeremo rubbed his temples. "You sure do. We've had it rough here. I've got to manage the food coming in from Crimonia, the distribution of the seafood—and—why'd I end up in this mess?"

"Because that's the kind of man you are. You work your butt off for the seaport."

Jeremo snorted. "I work hard? News to me...and to all the people who talk about me."

"I also know you've been kind to the townspeople."

"Bit of an overstatement."

"Oh, shut it. You're a good guy, Jeremo, and you always seem more surprised about it than everybody else."

Right then, Anabell—the guild worker from Crimonia—appeared. She seemed like a...hmm. How do I put it? Let's call her a thorough and inflexible woman.

Jeremo jumped. "Anabell?"

"You do try to skip out on work," she said, "but the townspeople like you. The moment I dropped your name and said you needed help, the lot of them were willing to lend a hand. They send you things, you know. Yes, I feel like I understand why the elders chose you to be the guild master." She tilted her head. Inexplicably, I thought of knives. "But I do wish you would stop skipping out on your work."

Jeremo offered a sheepish smile. "Uh, could we call this a break?"

"How many hours has it been, now, Jeremo?" Yep, that was a knife-look. "The future of this seaport rests on your shoulders."

"My delicate frame, you know, ah..." He cleared his throat. "I don't know if I could carry something quite so heavy."

"Then you're fine with the seaport going to ruin?"

"No, no. I'm simply saying that it could be someone else who does this. You, for instance."

Anabell shook her head. "If I were to do it, the seaport's revival would take ages. After all the disasters this place has suffered, they need someone they can trust. We both know that I'm not that person."

"And we both know that *I'm* not the greatest of—"

I broke in: "Quit it, Jeremo. You know who else trusts you? *Me.* Since I know it's you, I can entrust the fish I catch to the trade guild—no, to everyone here in seaport, working in harmony—without worrying."

Jeremo turned to me, bleary-eyed. He must've been pulling some rough all-nighters. "Damon, come on. Do I look like I'd actually be motived to work just because you said that?"

"Heh. No way." Jeremo and I burst into laughter.

He didn't look it, but Jeremo was a guy who got things done.

Later that day, I headed out to the ocean. A few other fishers sailed along with me—by coincidence—and on the gentle waves, we drifted past the place where the girl had slain the kraken. The gigantic backs of the bear statues loomed, and we sent our thanks.

The sea waited, with all of her bounty, and my heart swelled with gratitude that we could visit it once again in peace and safety.

Thank you.

Afterword

THANK YOU for picking up *Kuma Kuma Kuma Bear*'s sixth volume. Thanks to all of you, we've been able to smoothly reach the sixth book.

In this volume, Yuna goes to guard the students like she promised Ellelaura. Since she's in her bear outfit as usual, the students dismiss Yuna, but a strong monster appears before the students. The students risk their lives fighting it, but Yuna in her bear outfit has to be the one to defeat it. The guarding arc developments are a little different from the web version of the book, so I hope you enjoy them.

The latter half is about setting up the shop with Anz, who just came from Mileela. With Tiermina and Milaine's help, they fully set up the Bear Bistro.

After the shop opening goes off without a hitch, Yuna asks Fina to harvest the black tiger she slew in the guarding quest—but Fina's iron knife can't be used to harvest it. Yuna and Fina head to the capital to get a knife that can be used for the harvest. While there, Yuna accepts a new work quest. After this point, we get into the golem arc, which is continued in Volume 7. I hope you will wait until then.

Finally, I'd like to thank everyone who worked so hard to get this book out. Thank you for drawing such cute illustrations even while you were busy, 029. I always look forward to seeing what you produce.

I'm always causing trouble for my editor because of my typos and omissions. So, to the many people who were involved in the publishing of *Kuma Kuma Kuma Bear,* Volume 6, thank you.

I'm grateful for the readers who have read along thus far. I look forward to seeing you again in the seventh volume this coming July!

KUMANANO – ON A DAY IN MARCH, 2017